SPANISH TRYST

Beth Lindsay found herself stranded in Spain when her fiancé and employer, Patrick Neal, broke off their engagement. A chance encounter led her to employment with Perez Vineyards, headed by Vincente Perez, who had recently inherited the company in controversial circumstances. When Beth and Vincente went to Barcelona on business, an attraction flared between them. But Beth had reason to be wary of the secretive Spaniard . . .

JANET COOKSON

SPANISH TRYST

Complete and Unabridged

LINFORD
Leicester

First published in Great Britain in 2000

First Linford Edition
published 2001

British Library CIP Data

Cookson, Janet
  Spanish tryst.—Large print ed.—
Linford romance library
  1. Love stories
  2. Large type books
  I. Title
  823.9'14 [F]

  ISBN 0–7089–4568–6

Published by
F. A. Thorpe (Publishing)
Anstey, Leicestershire

Set by Words & Graphics Ltd.
Anstey, Leicestershire
Printed and bound in Great Britain by
T. J. International Ltd., Padstow, Cornwall

This book is printed on acid-free paper

1

Beth moved her chair to take advantage of the shade afforded by the brightly-coloured parasol, spread out the crumpled sheet of paper on the table before her, and, once more, read through the letter which spelled out the ruin of all her dreams.

Engrossed in her thoughts, she was unaware of the waiter hovering at her elbow until a discreet cough drew her eyes to Paolo's smiling face. As she took the glass of iced lemonade she had ordered she exchanged pleasantries in rapid Spanish but once he had gone she found her thoughts crowding in on her and her gaze wandered abstractedly around the small, harbourside café.

At this time, mid-September, the Spanish sun was as warm as ever but the hordes of tourists who normally thronged the small fishing village of

Puerto del Segura had now deserted it to return to homes and offices. The café, which Paolo ran with such friendly efficiency during the high season, was now empty save for herself and a man who had commandeered a table in the corner, his dark head bent over impressive-looking documents. He glanced up and as his dark brown eyes met hers Beth felt a sudden stab of recognition before hastily averting her gaze.

She wondered briefly why he seemed familiar but the next moment speculation flew out of her mind when a hand dropped on her shoulder and a voice with a Scottish lilt said, 'Hi! I'm sorry I'm so late. I persuaded Maria to look after the children whilst I popped out to see you but they made such a fuss when I tried to leave I had to wait until their morning nap.'

'That's all right,' Beth said, knowing how seriously Kirsty took her duties as an au pair, and, as her friend threw herself into a chair, her freckled face wreathed in smiles, she added, 'Oh, Kirsty, I'm so glad to see you.'

Immediately, Kirsty leaned forward, concern shadowing her face.

'What's the matter, Beth? You seemed terribly upset on the phone.'

'Everything's the matter.'

Beth flicked the sheet of paper in front of her with one finger tip.

'I received this letter yesterday from Patrick. In a few short lines, he has broken off our engagement!'

Kirsty's eyes rounded in contempt.

'You mean to say he didn't have the decency to face you in person, he just sent a letter?'

'Well, he is in London,' Beth pointed out, 'whilst I'm in Spain.'

'That doesn't excuse him,' Kirsty said with an indignant shake of her ginger curls. 'It's a lousy trick, Beth, and you know it.'

Inwardly Beth had to agree, yet Kirsty didn't know the half of it yet. She was just about to tell her when her friend pre-empted her with, 'But, Beth, how will this affect your job? Patrick was also your employer.'

The shrug of Beth's shoulders said it all.

'What job? The truth is that Patrick has fallen in love with my replacement, with the woman he hired to act as his assistant whilst I was here completing research for his next book.'

Kirsty's eyes flashed fire.

'So this woman has stolen your job as well as your fiancé!'

Beth's smile was resigned.

'I can hardly shift all the blame on to someone I don't know. It takes two, Kirsty. Obviously Patrick did not have the loyalty I believed him to have when I fell in love with him.'

'Obviously not! What will you do now. Will you return to London?'

'I'd like to, but for one awkward fact. I'm afraid I don't have enough money for the flight.'

'But why not? Surely it's Patrick's responsibility to fly you back. He sent you here.'

'It was part of the agreement,' Beth admitted. 'But under the circumstances I don't feel able to ask him for money.'

'But he owes it to you,' Kirsty protested. 'You're within your rights.'

'No! I don't wish to have any further contact with the man. I'll find the money myself.'

'How?'

'By working, of course. It might be out of season but there are plenty of cafés and bars that still need staff and my fluent Spanish will help.'

'You're seeking work in bars?' Kirsty repeated, bewildered. 'But you're an experienced personal assistant with language skills. Surely you can find something better.'

'I can't afford to be choosy. I'm stranded in a foreign country with very little money. I need to find work quickly.'

As her eyes wandered once more around the deserted café she wondered if she was being over-optimistic in thinking that Puerto del Segura's restaurants and cafés would provide her with the employment she so desperately needed. Paolo's other customer was still there, though, and he seemed to have lost all interest in the documents he had been reading. His head tilted to one side, a thoughtful expression on his face, and his eyes trained on herself and Kirsty. Had he been eavesdropping on their rather intimate conversation? She flashed him an indignant stare and this time it was his turn to avert his eyes. As his dark head lowered once more over his papers Kirsty's voice hissed in her ear.

'Good heavens, look who's there!'

'Who? I thought he seemed familiar but didn't know why.'

'Really, Beth, you've lived here for three months now and you don't recognise Vincente Perez? His face was plastered across the front of the local papers for weeks. His family owns a good many of the vineyards around here and when his uncle died recently they discovered he'd made Vincente sole heir, thereby disinheriting his own children. Of course that caused ructions and the children, a son and daughter, I believe, went to the media and alleged all sorts of double dealing. It all got rather nasty and the Press had a field day.'

'Did they go to court and resolve it there?' Beth asked.

'No. Apparently they came to some sort of arrangement. The unpleasant publicity has died down and, I presume, they've got on with the business of making wine.'

Beth's curious glance encompassed Vincente Perez once more. He cut an elegant figure in a lightweight suit the colour of pale champagne and she wondered aloud why he had chosen such a humble place as Paolo's café.

'Surely he would usually frequent the more upmarket restaurants in the Old Town?' she said.

'You would think so, wouldn't you?' Kirsty agreed.

Her orange juice arrived and her

attention was drawn away from further speculation as she gulped down the drink. Finishing with a sigh she pushed the empty glass away from her and addressed herself once more to her friend's plight.

'Look, I have a little money put by and you're welcome to that until you get back on your feet.'

'Oh, Kirsty, what a kind offer! I do appreciate it.'

Beth spoke with sincerity. She had got to know Kirsty shortly after the girl arrived in Puerto del Segura to take up a post as an au pair and Beth had increasingly come to appreciate her kindly nature. But she knew Kirsty earned little and had no intention of exploiting her generosity.

'I can't accept, though,' she went on. 'I'm young and strong and I'll soon find work. Don't you worry about me.'

She hoped she sounded more convincing than she felt but her reply seemed to satisfy Kirsty.

'If that's what you want I'll respect

your decision, but don't hesitate to ask me if you need any help.'

A glance at her watch had her rising abruptly to her feet.

'Look at the time! I need to get back and relieve the housekeeper.'

She deposited a kiss on Beth's cheek and, agreeing to meet again soon, they went their separate ways.

Deciding to go straight back to her apartment, Beth began to follow the narrow, winding lane which ran uphill through the Old Town. The street was full of local people buying at the market stalls which thronged the roadside and as she passed by her senses were assailed by the scents of newly-baked bread, different cheeses and the over-whelming smell of fish newly caught that morning.

At last, a little out of breath, she reached the building which housed her apartment. In spite of the rather grand baroque exterior, her flat consisted of two rather austere rooms on the top floor with the use of a shared bathroom on the landing outside. Its saving grace, as far as Beth was concerned, was that it did have a balcony, and, after making herself some strong coffee, she stepped on to it.

Leaning against the wrought-iron balustrade, she looked down on the panorama of red pantiled roofs jostling beneath a brilliant blue sky without really taking in the scene. Kirsty had been too polite to ask Beth why she was so short of money when she had been living cheaply in Spain and enjoying a generous salary for months and Beth had been in no mood to explain. She rarely spoke of her grandmother to anyone.

The onset of Alzheimer's disease which had taken her proud, strong-minded grandmother away from her had been such a shock she was still struggling to come to terms with it. Finding a nursing home run by an independent trust which ran an enlightened régime had done much to allay her fears for her grandmother's day-to-day comfort but good care came at a price, and, for the last year, most of Beth's salary had gone towards supplementing the fees. She had never resented one penny of it, for she owed her grandmother everything.

When her parents had first started working abroad and enrolled her in a boarding school, which had proved to be quite the wrong environment, it had been her grandmother who had answered her pleas for help. One Saturday morning, the old lady had simply arrived out of the blue and had informed the headmistress that she was removing her granddaughter forthwith as she would never thrive in her care.

But she had thrived in her grandmother's care and when her parents divorced and settled permanently abroad they became increasingly distant figures and her grandmother the focus of her world. How would she fulfil her financial obligations to her now without a well-paid job? Would work as a waitress bring in enough for both of them? It would have to, she decided, vowing to work all the hours there were to ensure that her grandmother would not suffer as a result of her present predicament.

She felt a moment of pure malice for the man who had dumped her in such a brutal manner and left her stranded in a foreign country. What on earth had she ever seen in Patrick Neal in the first place? The answer was easy, she had to admit to herself ruefully. With his blue eyes, shock of fair hair, and easy charm, he had had little difficulty in sweeping her off her feet. She had been impressed, too, by the way he had encouraged her to make full use of her knowledge of European languages so that soon she had been elevated from mere secretary to an assistant who did most of the research for the travel books which were his stock in trade.

They had worked well together and this harmony had been matched in their personal lives as they had fallen in love, or, at least, she had. Now that she had the benefit of knowing his true, fickle nature, she doubted that his feelings for her had ever run deep.

She let out a long sigh, then a glance at her watch pulled her up short. It would soon be lunchtime and the various restaurants and cafés clustered in the Old Town would be in the middle of their preparations. Now was the best time to speak to managers about work before they became too busy with their customers.

She hurried inside and took a cursory look at herself in the mirror where solemn blue eyes stared back at her. She took a brush to her thick mane of raven black hair but, as usual, found it difficult to tame the unruly curls into any semblance of order. Flinging the brush down she decided that prospective customers were not looking for a model girl but a hard-working waitress so she picked up her handbag and then hurried out, her heels tapping out a tattoo as she ran down the stairs.

She burst through the front door and cannoned straight into a tall man who was studying the brass nameplates attached to the wall. Large hands descended on to her shoulders and as she was held at arm's length she found herself looking into dark eyes and apologising for her clumsiness in breathless Spanish.

The hands dropped and he said in flawless English.

'That's quite all right, senorita. I was just about to ring your doorbell so was standing directly in your path.'

It was the man from the café and whilst questions spun around her mind as to why he should be seeking her out he gave an incline of the head and said, 'My name is Vincente Perez.'

'Beth Lindsay.'

A large, tanned hand enfolded hers briefly, but as questions rose to her lips he pre-empted her.

'You must excuse my unconventional approach but I was in the café where you and your friend were earlier and I

14

couldn't help but hear some of your conversation.'

So he had been eavesdropping! Beth's cheeks stained scarlet as she thought of what she and Kirsty had been discussing and her irritation prompted her next words.

'That conversation was private, Senor Perez.'

He held his hands up as though to ward off her criticism.

'I know and I'm sorry if I've upset you. It was quite unintentional. Only I think I might be of service to you.'

Oh, he did, did he, Beth thought sceptically. Well, there was something that needed clarifying before she listened to any more of his honeyed words.

'But how did you find me?' she asked, wondering, uneasily, if he had followed her all the way from the café.

He gave a shrug of his wide shoulders.

'As you seemed quite friendly with Paolo I asked him for your address and he was happy to supply it.'

'But he has no right to hand out my address to anyone who asks!'

A flush rose beneath Vincente's tanned cheeks.

'Paolo knows me very well as a respectable businessman, not as a stalker of young women. He was happy to entrust me with your address, especially when he knew my purpose in speaking to you.'

'Which is?' Beth asked, edgily.

'I wish to offer you work at my company, Perez Vineyards, in an administrative post. We need a native English speaker with fluent Spanish and you, Miss Lindsay, seem to fit the bill.'

Beth was lost for words. On the face of it it would seem to be the answer to her prayers. Yet her natural caution held her back from an immediate response. Vincente Perez was speaking again.

'We would, of course, offer you full hospitality at Casa Perez whilst you worked for us. As we are rather isolated it would not be possible for you to commute from Puerto del Segura every day, but — '

Beth held up a warning hand.

'Senor Perez! Before you re-organise my life any more I think it only fair to tell you that I have no intention of taking this any further. You are a complete stranger to me and, under those circumstances, I would not dream of taking up any job offer which entailed living in your house!'

Now he made no attempt to disguise his anger.

'If you insist on painting me as the sort of man who prowls the streets picking up young women with spurious excuses there's little I can do to defend myself. As this conversation is clearly getting us nowhere I will go.'

He turned abruptly and left, his long strides taking him quickly into the crowds of people milling about the street and out of view.

Perplexed, Beth mulled over their encounter. What an extraordinary turn of events! She had just been offered the job of her dreams but in circumstances in which she had felt obliged to refuse. And how arrogant of Vincente Perez to think that she would accept a job, and accommodation, from a complete stranger! Shaking her head she set off once more for the restaurant which was the first on her list.

Several hours later, she soaked in a hot bath back at her apartment and considered the humiliations of the afternoon. Of course, in the warm, Spanish way which she had grown to love, they had been sympathetic. She had received many complementary drinks, but no offers of work. The refrain had been the same in every place she had visited. Out of season, there was barely enough work to go around for their regular staff, let alone casual helpers. Trying to revive her spirits she resolved, first thing in the morning, to put an advertisement in the local paper offering English lessons.

A week later, no-one had replied to her advertisement, further enquiries at bars and cafés had proved fruitless, and she was currently seated at her dining-room table making an emergency audit of her meagre finances. As far as she knew the rent on the apartment was paid until the end of the month. Knowing that she had a roof over her head until then was the only bright spot in this whole sorry mess.

Next morning even that comfort was torn from her as she opened the door to find her landlady on the doorstep. She explained that the lease on the apartment had just run out and Senor Neal had not contacted her to renew it, but if the senorita could pay a month's rent in advance she would be happy to issue a new lease in the senorita's name.

Ashen faced, Beth invited her in and explained her position in the frankest terms promising to leave the next day so that the apartment could be let immediately. To her landlady's solicitous enquiries as to where she would go she explained that she had a friend who would happily accommodate her.

And that's all moonshine, she thought, as she showed out her landlady, as the only close friend she had in Puerto del Segura was Kirsty and she didn't think her employers would take too kindly to her putting up her English friend.

What on earth was she going to do? She spent a moment cursing the treacherous Patrick who had now ripped the roof from over her head with the same brutal indifference with which he had expelled her from his professional and personal life, then pulled herself up for wasting precious time on the rat when she needed to focus on what to do next. An image of the face of Vincente Perez rose before her. Dare she re-consider his proposal, and would he even agree to meet her after she had summarily dimissed him only a week ago? Perhaps the position he was seeking to fill was now taken, after all there were other expatriate English speakers in this part of Spain. Questions crowded her brain and Beth decided to sleep on it.

The next morning found her standing outside her apartment, her large suitcase which held all her worldly goods beside her, and her thoughts in disarray after a listless night. A strong cappuccino at a roadside café restored some sense of well-being and Beth found herself reaching the tentative conclusion that it would be foolish, given her dire situation, not to attempt, at least, to speak to Vincente Perez about the job he was offering. But how could she make contact with him when she had no idea where Casa Perez was and how to get there? The answer floated into her mind almost immediately. Paolo might well be able to help her.

She threw coins down on her table to pay for her drink and set off for the harbour, thankful that the route was downhill as her suitcase was heavy. When she arrived at the café she found Paolo enjoying a coffee with one of his waiters. He took one look at Beth's face, another look at the large suitcase she was carrying and then drew up a chair with a flourish.

Thankful to take the weight off her feet, Beth sat down and then the words tumbled out of her as she explained her predicament. Although clearly bemused, Paolo could tell her what she needed to know and began, immediately, to sketch out directions to Casa Perez on a paper serviette. It was quite a distance out of town and, knowing that she could not afford the taxi fare, Beth enquired about public transport. A bus would take her part of the way, Paolo informed her, and began to scribble down details and times.

She voiced her determination to go that afternoon and, to her relief, Paolo offered to store her suitcase for her until she had sorted herself out. After taking out a slim valise containing her references and CV she thanked him and left for the small bus station.

An hour later, her pessimism seemed to be justified as she was deposited at the dusty roadside and she looked around at a landscape devoid of any sign of habitation, the far horizon stretching endlessly before her. What she was looking at was typical of the countryside of the Gorgos valley with vineyards covering the valley floor and the soil, which could be glimpsed from the road, turning from red to yellow. She wondered if the rows of vines were part of the Perez estate and if that meant that she was not far from the family home.

As she smoothed out the serviette, now rather creased, she tried to recall exactly what advice Paolo had given her. Concluding that she needed to continue on the same road and then veer off to the right, Beth set off. She really was at the back of beyond, she decided, as she left the main road for the narrow lane which, according to the hastily-drawn map, would lead her to Casa Perez.

Thirty minutes later, Beth was beginning to think she was on the wrong road altogether and she stopped, pushed her straw sun hat back from her head and brushed back dampened curls from her forehead whilst she wondered what to do next. The heat was stifling, there was still no sign of her destination and not a single vehicle had passed her whilst she had been on this side road. She had only two choices, to continue for a little while longer or go back to the main road and ask for directions from a passing motorist.

Lost in her thoughts, not even the purring of a car engine distracted her and when a sleek, low-slung sports car rounded the bend behind her she had only seconds to leap out of the way, going over on one ankle and falling heavily on to the grassy verge. She remained in a heap, dazed and trying to catch her breath until a voice drew her eyes to a young man hovering solicitously over her.

'Senorita,' he repeated and when she turned puzzled, wide blue eyes to his and her sun hat fell back to reveal her dark curls he switched immediately to English. 'Are you hurt? Please, let me help you up.'

She took his proffered hand and was pulled gently to her feet. As she began to dust herself down he began to apologise.

'Please, do not apologise, senor. The mishap was all my fault. I was standing in the middle of the road and not paying attention at all.'

His face broke into a charming smile.

'We won't quarrel about it, senorita, at least not until we've been properly introduced.'

He held out his hand once more.

'I am Juan Perez.'

Her pulse leaped at the sound of his name and as she took his hand she said, 'Beth Lindsay.'

'Well, Beth Lindsay,' he responded, his head tilted and his brown eyes twinkling, 'may I ask what you are doing here, alone?'

'I'm looking for Casa Perez as I wish to speak to Vincente Perez on a business matter. Do I take it that he is a relative of yours?'

Juan made a mock formal bow.

'I am delighted to say he is my cousin.'

He did not sound at all delighted and Beth, remembering what Kirsty had said, realised now that she must be addressing one of the disinherited children. That was not something Beth wanted to be drawn into so she spoke quickly.

'I hope you don't think me ill-mannered for seeking out your cousin at your family home unannounced only I need to speak to him urgently.'

'My sister, Juanita, is home at the moment and we shall be very pleased to receive you at Casa Perez. Come, Beth.'

He motioned for her to follow him to his car which was parked, slightly askew, farther up the lane but as she put her weight full on to her left foot pain shot through her ankle and she stumbled. Juan was immediately by her side as she explained.

'I wrenched it a little when I fell over. I don't think it's at all serious.'

She was quite prepared to hobble to the car but he had other ideas and swung her up into his arms, in spite of her protests. Having ensconced her into the passenger seat, he turned to her with a smile.

'We shall be at Casa Perez in a few, short minutes.'

Next moment he had gunned the engine and Beth realised he would be as good as his word as the car set off at breakneck speed.

2

After passing through a gateway marked by two white pillars and an archway with the name Casa Perez woven into the wrought iron, they continued down a drive flanked by orange trees and drew to a halt in front of a two-storeyed villa in white with a red pantiled, pitched roof, bougainvillaea-draped balconies breaking up the long, low frontage.

With a smile designed to take the sting out of her refusal, Beth declined to be carried into Casa Perez but did accept Juan's arm and limped inside to find the interior of the house blessedly cool. The hallway, with its terracotta floor tiles and dark furniture carved in traditional manner, was typical of many of the houses she had seen in Valencia, although more luxuriously appointed. She was deposited on a chair by Juan who told her he would send the housekeeper to her to administer a little first aid to her ankle.

Before Beth could protest that her ankle was feeling better already, he had gone, shortly to be replaced by a middle-aged, smiling woman who, when Beth greeted her in Spanish, chatted away happily as she checked over Beth's ankle with the professional air of the nurse she had once been. Announcing herself satisfied that Beth had only suffered a mild wrench which required no further attention, she departed and Beth rose and took a few experimental steps, noting with relief that her left ankle was now able to bear her weight.

'Carla assures me that you will live!'

Beth turned to find Juan, his hands resting on his hips, watching her, eyes twinkling.

'I'm pleased to hear it,' she said in the same light-hearted tone.

'I've told Juanita we have a guest so, come, Beth, and meet my sister.'

He led her through a charming lounge on his right and out through tall windows folded back to allow the sun to pour through on to a terrace dotted with sun loungers and tables. A girl was leaning against the balustrade and as she walked forward to greet them, Beth looked from her to Juan in astonishment. Her ebony curls, so similar to her brother's, framed a face which was identical to his, even down to the dimple which marked her chin.

'You're twins!' Beth burst out and they laughed.

'Most people are quite shocked when they see us together for the first time,' Juanita confirmed. 'Although we are identical, with us being different genders, people seem to expect more of a difference. Anyway, enough about us. Welcome to Casa Perez, Beth,' she added with a smile.

Beth shook the extended hand.

'I'm glad to be here,' she confided. 'When Juan came across me, I had just convinced myself I was on the wrong road and needed to turn back.'

'Juan tells me you travelled out from Puerto del Segura in order to speak to my cousin, Vincente. Do you know my cousin well?'

'I've only met him once and that was briefly. It's rather a strange story. You see, your cousin offered me a job and I refused. Now I wish to see if he will reconsider his offer.'

Juanita's brows rose.

'This sounds as though my rather austere cousin had been acting out of character. I'm intrigued. Join us for refreshments, Beth, and tell us about it.'

There was a jug of iced, freshly-squeezed orange juice on one of the tables and when Carla, the house-keeper, brought an extra glass and some sandwiches, Beth found herself suddenly ravenous as she bit into warm, crusty bread. Soon they were chatting away like old friends. Beth found the twins remarkably easy to talk to and, leaving out the part that Patrick had been her fiancé as well as her boss,

31

relayed all that had happened to her over the last turbulent week. When she had finished, Juanita seemed even more surprised by Vincente's behaviour.

'No offence to you, Beth, but I am rather astonished that Vincente should offer work to someone he met in a café. Usually he's so cautious.'

'So am I. That's why I turned him down flat,' Beth responded.

'Well, I'm glad you decided the Perez family was worth a second look.'

Juan made a mock salute with his glass of orange juice, his glance one of open admiration and Beth found her cheeks warming with a blush.

'Besides,' he said, turning to his sister, 'the business really could do with a native English speaker at the moment. Our trade with the States and the UK is growing fast. Beth would be a real asset.'

'I'm sure she would be,' Juanita returned diplomatically. 'I just find Vincente's recruiting methods rather odd.'

Beth did, too, but when she enquired as to when she would be able to see Vincente, she was met with shrugged shoulders.

'He's due back from Madrid today,' Juan told her, 'but we've no idea when to expect him.'

Juanita looked at her watch, then rose, saying, 'Well, it's siesta time now so I'll show you to a guest bedroom. You can freshen up, rest, and we'll all meet up later.'

The room which Juanita led her into was spacious, with a huge bed with a carved, wooden headboard facing a central seating area where a small sofa in crimson damask, with matching velvet scatter cushions, was flanked by coffee tables. Walking over to the cabinets fitted against the far wall, Juanita opened one door to reveal a fridge stacked with a variety of drinks.

'Feel free to take what you want. The bathroom's through there and there are plenty of towels. I do hope you'll be comfortable here, Beth.'

Beth thought she sounded as though she expected her to stay at Casa Perez for some time. She, herself, thought there were little grounds for such optimism and as she thanked Juanita and was left alone she was once more assailed by doubts as to the wisdom of arriving here out of the blue. How was Vincente Perez going to respond when they were face to face? Only a week ago she had dismissed his job offer out of hand and now she was bearding him in his home to see if she could reconsider her decision.

After showering she lay down on the bed in her underclothes for a short rest but within minutes she had slipped into a deep sleep, exhausted by the tensions of the day and the midday heat. She woke with a shock some time later and, after scrambling into her dress, set off in search of her hosts.

Carla directed her towards the swimming pool and she retraced her earlier footsteps but, instead of lingering on the terrace, crossed it and descended a set of steps which led to a huge swimming pool where Juan and his sister were frolicking in the water. They waved to Beth and then got out to join her. Beth could see a jug of home-made lemonade, with glasses, set out on one of the tables and she began to pour the drinks, the twins joining her after a brisk rub down with towels.

'Thanks,' Juanita said, accepting the offered glass, adding, 'I do hope you had a good rest, Beth.'

'I fell into a really deep sleep,' she admitted, then went on, a little self-consciously. 'I'm really grateful for your hospitality but I almost feel as though I'm accepting it on false pretences at the moment. After all, I have no real reason to be here, until I've spoken to your cousin that is.'

Juanita dismissed her concerns with a wave of her tiny hand.

'Oh, there's no need to stand on formalities with us, Beth. For my part I'm delighted to have some female company. Normally I'm outnumbered at Casa Perez.'

'That's not quite true, twin,' Juan put in, a mischievous edge to his voice. 'We do enjoy frequent visits from the lovely Diane.'

They burst out laughing and Beth, wondering what the joke was, was enlightened by Juan.

'Without sounding too unkind, we believe that Diane is a little unfinished business from our cousin's years in California.'

Eyes twinkling, Juanita continued the tale.

'You see, Vincente learned the wine trade in the new world. He only came to Spain a few months before our father died. Not long after his arrival, the glamorous Diane rented a neighbouring villa. She and Vincente were apparently close in the States and she lost no time in rekindling the relationship once she had moved there. She's supposed to be starting up some new business but seems to do very little beyond groom herself and dance attendance on our cousin.'

Clearly they had little time for Vincente's glamorous companion but that was not a subject Beth wanted to go into right now. Their comments had satisfied her curiosity on one point, though.

'Your cousin's years in California would explain his flawless English,' she remarked.

'Oh, Vincente is half English,' Juan informed her. 'His mother came to this area as an au pair and when she returned to England, Uncle Esteban followed her and they married. Vincente was born and brought up there. They didn't move to the States until he was a teenager.'

'There have always been strong connections with England in our family,' Juanita said. 'Our grandmother was English and when our mother died, after giving birth to us, Father employed an English nanny to look after us.'

'We spoke English before we spoke Spanish,' Juan said, taking up the tale, 'and later on we were sent to summer school in Brighton every year to polish up our skills.'

Juanita finished her drink, placed the glass on the table and then suggested they have another swim.

'Are you going to join us?' she asked Beth.

'Well, no, I can't,' Beth demurred, and when Juan enquired solicitously if her ankle still troubled her she shook her head. 'No. It's still a little sore, but nothing to worry about. But I don't have a swimsuit with me!'

Juanita dismissed her concerns with a shake of her head.

'There are plenty of spare bikinis in the summer house. Come, Beth.'

Beth had no option but to comply, although she had some doubts about joining in with a family bathing party when she had come to Casa Perez simply to apply for a job. She had even greater misgivings when she saw the suits on offer which were all two-pieces and tiny.

She finally settled for one in a bold cerise colour which, although more revealing than one she would have picked for herself, was modest compared with what else was on offer. It was glorious to be in the warm water of the swimming pool and as Beth completed one length after another she felt the cares of the day and the memory of the hot and dusty journey fading. Juan and Juanita began a strenuous game with a beach ball and when Beth joined in, it quickly descended into a noisy frolic as the twins squabbled about the rules, although, as far as Beth could see, no rules existed!

At last, tired, Beth declared she had had enough and began to climb out of the pool. Juan followed and, in tones of mock gallantry, declared that he would carry her to the summer house to change as she had injured her ankle earlier. Laughingly, Beth insisted that she was fine but Juan, ignoring her protestations, picked her up and swung her high into the air. She was still voicing her protest and Juan was, jokingly, still refusing to let her go when a volley of words, in rapid Spanish, broke into their exchange.

'My cousin says I must put you down, Beth,' Juan said, pulling a face.

Her head shot round to find Vincente Perez at the base of the steps leading to the house, his jacket slung over his shoulder, a small, leather suitcase in one hand. His dark eyes widened as he took in her features.

'Miss Lindsay! I'd no idea it was you my cousin was holding captive. How pleasant to see you at Casa Perez.'

As the words were spoken with chilly disdain Beth doubted that very much but his tone was little warmer when he went on.

'Are you here for purely social reasons or is there another purpose?'

Self-consciously, Beth pushed wet hair out of her eyes, uncomfortably aware that water still streamed from her and that her hair was plastered to her head like a skull cap. This was not the way she had planned to meet her prospective employer and as she stammered out her response she was acutely aware of what a ridiculous figure she must be cutting.

'I wished to speak to you about the job you mentioned a week ago.'

'The one you even refused to consider?'

'Yes,' Beth admitted, adding hurriedly, 'but I've had second thoughts and wondered if you're willing to give me a few moments of your time.'

'I'll see you in my office in one hour.'

He threw the words over his shoulder as he ran up the steps, leaving Beth to stare after him in consternation.

'Don't worry about Vincente,' Juanita said consolingly. 'It's just his manner. Underneath he's, well, he's — '

'Much worse,' Juan quipped, until a warning glance from his sister silenced him.

'I can't blame him for being a little stand-offish with me,' Beth said. 'Last week I cut him dead when he wanted to offer me work and now he comes back from a trip and finds me frolicking in his pool. He must think I'm a complete airhead.'

'Well, you've got a chance to impress him when he interviews you,' Juanita said, but her words, intended to reassure, merely rang alarm bells in Beth's mind.

'My dress is dusty from the journey, I've no other clothes with me, and my hair's going to be a complete mess after this dip in the pool. I really shall look a fright!'

'Beth! Calm yourself! I will find you something to wear and I'll even do your hair for you. Come, Beth,' Juanita insisted.

If Beth had doubts about the sort of clothes Juanita would deem suitable for an interview they were dispelled when she slid back the door of one of the fitted wardrobes in her room to reveal ranks of suits beautifully tailored in linen and ranging in shades from pastels to strong, primary colours.

'Father bought me these,' Juanita confided, 'but I rarely wear them, so, please, choose anything you like.'

Beth picked a suit in cornflower blue to match her eyes and Juanita suggested teaming it with a white, silky, cross-over blouse. Sheer stockings and high-heeled shoes completed the outfit and then Juanita asked Beth to sit in front of her dressing-table. Beth watched, transfixed, as Juanita drew her long, unruly curls back from her forehead with a wire brush, plaited them into a single pleat which she then wound into a coil at the nape of her neck, holding it in place with strong grips. It was a definite Spanish style and as Beth moved her head from side to side she realised, with delight, that it complemented her features and added an air of elegance.

'It's wonderful,' she breathed. 'I can't thank you enough, Juanita.'

As she checked her appearance one

last time in Juanita's full-length mirror she could only be thankful to her new-found friend for boosting her self confidence. At least Vincente Perez could not fault her appearance even if he did, in the end, decide not to employ her. A glance at the clock sent her scurrying out of the room.

The door of Vincente's office was half open and he motioned her inside with an impatient gesture, a glance at his watch giving the distinct impression that he did not approve of any unpunctuality, however slight.

'I see you have brought me your CV. Good. Excuse me a moment whilst I glance through it.'

Whilst he scanned each page Beth found herself subjecting him to covert scrutiny. It was difficult to believe that his mother had been English. There was no hint of fairer colouring in his strong, tanned features or in the gleaming, jet-black hair which brushed the collar of his crisp white shirt. His eyes, too, were sinfully dark, and were now looking right at her! As she attempted, unsuccessfully, to avert her gaze before his eyes locked with hers she had the uncanny feeling that he knew that he had been the subject of her curiosity. His eyes lowered once more.

'You seem to have had quite a variety of jobs, Miss Lindsay,' he commented.

'I suppose I have,' she said, a little flustered. 'I believe the experience has made me quite versatile,' she added.

'I agree,' he replied and Beth breathed a sigh of relief.

He leaned back in his chair, his features schooled into an expressionless mask.

'I'll be straight with you. You have the language skills I require but I'm also looking for someone who can take on responsibility and demonstrate initiative. Are you that person, Miss Lindsay?'

'I believe I am, senor.'

She didn't add that she was desperate for a job, any job, and in the silence that followed she wondered if he was well aware of that, having eavesdropped, somewhat shamefully, on her conversation in the café. How much had he heard?

'I would like to employ you on a trial basis, Miss Lindsay. Would a month's trial suit?'

She found herself nodding in assent. His mention of a starting salary, generous even by the standards she was used to, prompted her into words.

'I really am most grateful for the opportunity you are giving me, senor.'

He smiled, for the first time since she had entered the room, softening his features so that, for a moment, Beth was given a glimpse of his charm.

'You may not feel quite so grateful when you see the punishing schedule I have set out for you. I am frequently accused of being a workaholic and of expecting the same high standards from my staff. I hope, nevertheless, that we can forge a good working relationship. Let us shake hands on that.'

Beth took the proffered hand and, for

no accountable reason, found herself blushing as his hand encompassed hers. On leaving the office, Beth was pounced on by Juanita and when she passed on her good news her new friend whooped her delight.

'I'm so glad you'll be staying on here, Beth. It'll be wonderful to have someone to share girl talk with.'

Later, as Beth dressed for dinner in an elegant black dress loaned by Juanita, she marvelled at how quickly friendship had sprung up between herself and the twins. They had such an open, easy manner it was difficult not to warm to them immediately, unlike their cousin, whose cool, distant manner discouraged easy familiarity. Of course Vincent Perez had been brought up in a different culture and, if the rumours were to be believed, had found himself at the centre of a vicious family dispute. Perhaps his formidable self-possession was a product of the struggle to retain a family inheritance many would say he had no right to.

A glance at her watch sent her hurrying off in the direction of the dining-room but when she arrived she found it empty. The doors leading to the terrace were open, though, and when she wandered through she spied a tall woman with auburn hair leaning against the parapet, drink in hand. She turned at Beth's approach, her green eyes widening as she took in Beth's appearance. She straightened, her expression now shuttered as she offered her hand.

'Hi, I'm Diane Preston, a friend of Vincente. You must be the new secretary.'

'Beth Lindsay,' Beth replied, shaking the other woman's extended hand.

'I'm surprised Vincente managed to persuade you to come to work at Casa Perez,' Diane went on and when Beth looked at her in surprise she elaborated further. 'Well, it's not exactly sweetness and light here, is it? Vincente and the twins are at daggers drawn. They're convinced he sweet-talked their old man into disinheriting them when he was suffering from the final stages of a brain tumour and Vincente is equally convinced the twins briefed the Press against him and tried to ruin his reputation.'

'I'm not sure I should be listening to all this,' Beth stammered.

Diane waved her glass in Beth's face.

'I'm not telling you anything that's secret, honey. The whole neighbourhood's been discussing nothing else for months.'

'That's no reason why I should,' Beth pointed out.

'Just putting you straight for your own good, honey. If you're going to work for the Perez family you need to make sure you don't get caught up in the crossfire.'

As Diane began to weave unsteadily back towards the house, Beth realised that the other woman was a little the worse for drink. For the first time since she had accepted her new position Beth was beset by doubts.

3

The following day was Beth's first day at work and when she arrived at the office she found Vincente already busy.

'We begin work very early in Spain,' he explained, 'in order to take advantage of the coolest part of the day. We break for siesta after lunch and then return to our desks early evening. I'm sure you'll soon get used to it.'

Beth assured him that she would.

'I noticed in your CV that you've worked for a publisher as a proof-reader. These proofs,' he said, pointing to a stack of papers on the desk, 'relate to advertising material intended for the English-speaking market. They were translated from Spanish to English by the advertising agency and, I'm afraid, it's all turned out rather stilted. Please go through them and change them to clear, conversational English. I shall be out for the rest of the day, but you should have enough work to keep you occupied. I daresay I shall see you this evening.'

With those words, he was gone. Not having had an opportunity to ask questions Beth hoped that her task would prove as easy as he had airily supposed. Once she began her work, however, she quickly became engrossed. Vincente had been right in deriding the copy as stilted.

She began to re-write large chunks of prose and, lost in her work, was astonished to find, when she did look at her watch, that it was way past lunchtime. Carla would have served lunch and cleared away by now and Beth was acutely aware of a yawning hunger. There was a bowl of fruit in her room and that would have to do, she decided.

On reaching her room, she was pleased to see that Juan had been true to his word and had fetched her suitcase from Puerto del Segura. She unpacked quickly, relieved to find that her clothes were not too crumpled and, after showering, slipped into a lilac cotton dress with shoe-string straps before stepping out on to the terrace for a moment. Nothing stirred. It was siesta time for the whole house and as the fierce heat met her she gave a mental vote of thanks for this Mediterranean custom.

Returning indoors, she closed the shutters to keep the room cool but switched on her bedside light so that she could read. Picking up a light paperback she snacked on some fruit as she read but the insubstantial food did little to quell the hunger pangs and she was just thinking of going downstairs and raiding the fridge in the kitchen when her eyelids began to droop. The next moment she was fast asleep.

She woke with a shock, her neck stiff from the awkward angle in which she had dozed, and her throat parched. With a glance at her bedside clock she was prompted to hurry to the bathroom to splash cold water on her face in a bid to waken her sluggish senses. She had slept for far too long! She set off for the office, getting there in double quick time and coming to an abrupt halt as she entered to find Vincente sitting casually on the corner of her desk, arms folded.

'There you are, Beth. I wondered when you'd arrive.'

Beth rushed into words.

'I'd no intention of falling asleep, and then when I did I slept too long!'

'There's no need to apologise, it's not a crime to take a siesta. What I meant was that I've been waiting to see you, in order to congratulate you on what you've done. No need to look surprised. I do compliment my staff when it's deserved, you know. Anyway the changes you've made to the copy are quite justified. Tomorrow, I'll unearth some more translations I'm not particularly happy with and you can wield the red pen on those.'

'But my intention was to continue

tonight. There's time before dinner.'

'I don't think you need worry about the evening shift. Juanita mentioned that you missed lunch. Did you work through?'

When Beth admitted she had he surprised her by saying, 'Then you'll be starving and ready for an early supper. What do you say about joining me at a local restaurant?'

A tête-à-tête with the formidable Vincente was not her idea of a perfect evening but she knew any refusal had to be couched in diplomatic terms.

'Won't the others expect us here for dinner?' she queried. 'I wouldn't want to put Carla out at all.'

'No problem, Beth. What you must understand is that Casa Perez is a little like a hotel. We come and go as we please and I can assure you that the admirable Carla always copes. Of course I don't wish to impose myself on you. Perhaps you would find my company too irksome.'

Now how was she supposed to

respond to that? His dark eyes seemed to be issuing a challenge and she found herself saying defensively, 'I'd be happy to go out to supper with you, Senor Perez.'

'Good, although now we are working together please drop the formalities and call me Vincente.'

'As you wish . . . Vincente.'

Amusement fleeted across his face.

'Now that's settled, let's go.'

Beth had to hurry to keep up with his long strides. When they reached his car, an open-topped model in bronze, he opened the passenger door for her and Beth found herself settling into soft suede the colour of ivory.

As he brought the engine to life he said, 'I thought we'd drive up into the mountains and eat at a small restaurant I'm particularly fond of.'

As they set off at a rapid pace, Beth's reply was lost to the wind and as her hair streaked behind her she consoled herself with the thought that at least she wouldn't have to make small talk on the journey. Vincente handled the vehicle deftly but as they gained height and the countryside fell away on either side, the road narrowed and became more tortuous and Beth found herself gripping the edge of her seat. A building loomed up on their right, a few tables and chairs at the front protected by a striped awning. Vincente drew the car to a halt outside but, instead of stopping at one of the tables, drew her inside and motioned towards the stairs.

'Go up to the roof terrace, Beth, whilst I have a word with Pablo.'

She did as she was bid and when she moved to the parapet to look at the view found the breath catching in her throat. She hardly dared look down from this dizzying height but when she allowed herself a peek she saw sandy-coloured rock falling away sharply to a valley floor speckled with red roofed buildings which looked as though they had come from a child's building kit. She watched, fascinated, as a bird with a huge wing span hovered silently. It dropped suddenly out of sight and she turned to find Vincente behind her carrying a large tray.

'You seem engrossed in the view,' he commented.

She spread her hands wide.

'Who wouldn't be? It's magnificent here.'

He smiled, showing white, even teeth.

'I'm pleased you like it. Now, to dinner.'

He unloaded the tray on to a table clothed in a red checked table-cloth.

'I saved the senora's legs by bringing up our tapas so, come, eat, Beth.'

Ravenous, Beth needed no further bidding. The tapas consisted of a delicious selection of shellfish, olives and salads and to drink there were the traditional glasses of cognac.

'Have you eaten much of the local cuisine since you've been in Spain?' Vincente asked.

'Oh, yes, although not having transport has meant that I've been pretty well limited to the coastal region. I must say I've thoroughly enjoyed the food. The fish you eat has usually been caught that morning and the vegetables are just as fresh and tasty.'

'I was brought up by the sea, so I've always eaten fish as my staple diet!'

Reaching absentmindedly for an olive, Beth wondered if she dared risk a personal question.

'Which part of England was that? The twins told me you were born and brought up there,' she added in a rushed explanation.

He seemed unconcerned by her prior knowledge.

'Cornwall, not far from St Ives. Mum was a Cornish girl. She met her future husband when she came to this area as an au pair. When she returned to England he followed and they married. Although I only knew Cornwall I was brought up to be bi-lingual and Dad ensured that I knew all about my Spanish heritage.'

'Did you visit Casa Perez often when

you were a youngster?'

'Never. My first visit was six months before Uncle Felipe died.'

Beth was astonished and, without thinking, the words jumped out of her.

'But why? Was there some sort of family rift?'

Vincente's expression tightened.

'My father and Uncle Felipe had some sort of falling out and from the moment Dad left Spain they broke off relations. Other relatives would pass on news to us but direct contact was never made. Thankfully, I was able to be reconciled with my uncle before his death.'

And to walk off with the family business, Beth added mentally. No wonder the twins felt such resentment. A cousin they had never met had turned up out of the blue, and, from their point of view, had stolen their inheritance. She couldn't help feeling, as well, that Vincente was concealing a good deal. But then, why not? He hardly knew her. She was a lowly employee who had been working for him for precisely one day and that was hardly grounds for a heart to heart! Further speculation ceased as a smiling, middle-aged woman arrived with their main course.

'I took the liberty of ordering for you,' Vincente remarked, as a shallow, steaming dish was placed before Beth. 'It's a traditional dish called zarzuela, basically a fish stew, but it is delicious. Don't take my word for it,' he urged, as she picked up her fork and began to toy with her food. 'Try it.'

Several mouthfuls later she was able to compliment him on his choice.

'It's extraordinarily tasty. Why can't I ever cook fish in a way that enhances the delicate flavour?'

He smiled.

'People from the Mediterranean area seem to be born with cooking skills we can only dream of.'

Surprised at the remark, Beth wondered if he still saw himself as an outsider. To the casual observer he would appear to be no different from any other successful Spanish business-man and there was nothing in his manner or easy use of the Spanish language to reveal an upbringing far away. She gave abrupt voice to her curiosity.

'You sound as if you still feel a little detached from the culture here.'

Immediately she wished the words unsaid but he appeared to have taken no offence.

'I do feel at home here but I guess I just have to accept that I am rather a strange mixture. Throughout my child-hood I was just another Cornish boy. I felt slightly embarrassed about having a foreign dad and never spoke Spanish in front of my friends. Later on I learned to cherish my heritage and when we moved to California there were so many Hispanic people there that the two parts of me could co-exist quite happily. The move enabled Dad to buy the vineyard he'd always dreamed of and that meant I could learn the

61

business that has run in the Perez family for generations. The family joke, Beth, is that wine runs in our veins, not blood.'

The coffee came and, as Beth stirred the rich, dark liquid, she wondered how the twins were feeling now that the birthright which he had spoken of so eloquently had been taken from them.

'And do the twins share your passion for the business?' she began cautiously but, as his expression froze, she found her voice trailing away.

'The twins have a passion for the return it brings,' he said brusquely, adding, 'They haven't suffered financially from the changed will, you know. I make both of them a generous allowance which puts them in the fortunate position of enjoying a good income without having to work for it.'

'I really don't know anything about all of this,' Beth mumbled, embarrassed.

'I'm sure you've heard the rumours,' he put in, 'that I gained the Perez vineyards through dishonest means.'

'I have heard that there was some sort of family dispute,' she admitted. 'But I don't think I should get involved.'

He gave a wry smile.

'As you're living and working at Casa Perez you might find it difficult to remain detached, Beth.'

Was that the reason he had brought her out to dine tonight, to put forward his side of the story before she became too close to the twins? Her suspicions were fuelled further by his next words.

'The twins are charming people, both with the knack of making friends easily. But, Juan leads a rather feckless life. He's well-known in all the local bars, is tremendously popular, but, especially when he's drunk a little, is not known for his discretion.'

Beth felt anger rising within her at the casual way in which Vincente had just trashed his cousin's reputation.

'That's a harsh indictment of your cousin.'

He was unrepentant.

'I don't believe so. What I said can apply to many a young man who hasn't yet settled down in life. Unfortunately, Juan's tactlessness could cost us dear. We're in a wine-growing area, Beth, surrounded by rival vineyards and business is cutthroat. I simply can't have Juan rambling on about confidential business matters when he's in a bar. I want your assurance, Beth, that you will not discuss any of our business affairs with the twins.'

Now she knew the real reason why he had organised this cosy meal out. He wanted her help in freezing out his cousins! Her first instinct was to tell him that he was behaving despicably but, as caution re-asserted itself, she reminded herself that she knew little of the complex family situation she found herself in and that Vincente was, above all, her employer.

'You will always be able to rely on my discretion,' she said stiffly.

If he sensed her disapproval he

showed little sign of it, his features lightening as he broke into a smile.

'Good. I'm glad that's cleared the air between us.'

Beth found it difficult to settle back into the rôle of dinner guest after their unsettling conversation and was glad that, when she refused a dessert, the evening came to a speedy end and they set off back to Casa Perez. As they entered the house they were accosted immediately by Diane, and Beth wondered if she had been watching out for their return all evening.

'Come and have a night cap, darling.'

One tanned arm was wound through his and Vincente was carried off as Beth was completely ignored and then left alone in the hallway. She decided to go straight up to her room but once there it felt too early to go to bed so she switched on the lamp which illuminated the balcony and settled herself down with a book. She found it difficult to concentrate, however, and ended up flinging it down on the table as her mind began to pick over the events of the strange evening. She couldn't help feeling that there had been a menacing undertone to everything Vincente had said.

He seemed to be warning her against forming a close friendship with the twins, his views on Juan being particularly scathing. But why should she take any notice? He had no right to decide her friendships for her and he could hardly claim the moral high ground as he had inherited the family business under decidedly suspicious circumstances. Now feeling indignant at the way he appeared to have manipulated her into siding with him against his relatives Beth felt that she should have asserted her right not to involve herself in the tangled relationships of the Perez family. After all, she had been employed as a personal assistant, not as a mediator!

'Beth, hi! How are you?'

Juan's voice floated up towards her and she looked curiously over the balcony to find him standing below, eyes bright as he blew a kiss up to her.

'What on earth are you doing hanging around in the dark?' she hissed.

'Really, Beth, I am not hanging around, as you put it,' he admonished her. 'I am here to tell you how beautiful you look in moonlight.'

'You can't really see me from that angle!'

'Beth, you have no romance in you. I will have to take you in hand.'

Next moment, to Beth's astonishment, and before she could utter a word of protest, he was scrambling up the gnarled and twisted branches of the wisteria which covered the wall. She stepped back as his face appeared.

As he vaulted over the low, wrought-iron balustrade she said accusingly, 'You're mad! Why didn't you just walk up the stairs?'

A smile wreathed his features as he collapsed in a chair.

'But you wouldn't have let me in if

I'd come knocking at your door, would you?'

'No, I would not,' she said.

She ought to be angry with him but it was difficult keeping up any pretence of annoyance when faced with his engaging effrontery.

'Now you are here you'd better have a drink,' she went on, disappearing inside to choose something from the small, well-stocked fridge.

At the sight of the tall tumbler of fresh orange juice his face fell a little.

'Nothing stronger?' he queried.

'Oh, yes,' she returned smoothly, 'but I suspect you've already had enough to drink tonight.'

He pulled a face.

'I had to drown my sorrows just a little, you know, Beth, when I discovered that you'd gone out to dinner without me. How could you?'

'Very easily.' Beth laughed. 'I was asked.'

'I suppose Vincente is a better bet than me,' he went on slyly, 'and he is your boss, after all.'

'Yes, he is,' Beth said, firmly, wondering, momentarily, if Juan was quite as merry as he appeared. 'And I went out to dine with him as a courtesy, that's all.'

'You certainly upset Diane. She was quite livid.'

The thought seemed to please Juan, a broad grin crossing his face.

'No-one has reason to be angry about an innocent supper.'

'Was it all quite so innocent?'

Juan seized her right hand and she found herself pulled towards him.

'What did you talk about during this tête-à-tête. Did he mention anything about me and Juanita, or Papa?'

'No!'

She wrenched her hand away form him and stood up, irritated.

'Juan, I think you've had a little too much to drink and should go now.'

He covered his face with his hands, sounding genuinely mortified.

'Beth, I am so sorry. Everything in

life has been turned upside down recently and I guess it's turned me a little crazy.'

Mollified, Beth said, 'I think I understand, but I still think you should go.'

He jumped to his feet and went to the door but as she was letting him out he turned to her once more.

'Am I forgiven?'

He looked so woebegone that, acting purely out of instinct, she answered in the form of a gentle kiss placed on his lips. It was a mistake. As soon as her lips touched his, his arm snaked around her and she was crushed against him as he sought her lips in a much fiercer kiss. She had little choice but to capitulate for that brief moment and, after releasing her, he gave her a look of pure satisfaction before sauntering off.

She berated herself inwardly for being such a fool, when a soft sound alerted her and she turned to look back down the passageway in time to see a door close. She was unable to identify the tall figure who had been standing there but she had little doubt. It was Vincente's private suite and he would have had a perfect view of the scene between herself and his cousin.

4

After a fitful sleep Beth found herself waking in the early hours and, after rising and slipping on her robe, she settled herself on the balcony and watched the sun rise, her thoughts dominated by what had happened the day before. Although she had no desire to be drawn into the family feud which had been set in train by Felipe Perez changing his will she seemed to be getting involved in spite of herself.

Whilst accepting that she did not know all the complexities of the case her natural sympathies were with the twins who seemed to have been cheated. The evening she had spent with Vincente had shown the extent of the distrust between himself and his cousins and, although she had been happy to reassure him with the promise of her professional discretion, she had felt distinctly uncomfortable when he had implied that Juan was not to be trusted. He had virtually warned her off from intimate contact with him, so, what must he have thought when he had seen them in a clinch several hours later?

It had all the markings of a terrible mess, yet she could hardly blame Juan for taking her in his arms as she had foolishly instigated it! After her bruising dismissal by Patrick, though, she was in no mood for another emotional involvement and a dalliance with Juan was out of the question. She must set boundaries in their relationship, she decided, and she must show Vincente she was a conscientious employee and could be trusted.

She showered, dressed and hurried down to breakfast. Carla had set the table outside on the sunlit terrace and Beth was relieved to see Juanita sitting there alone. She greeted Beth's arrival with a smile.

' 'Morning, Beth. Carla's bringing

some fresh coffee but there's orange juice and croissants. Oh, and I have a message from Vincente,' she added, as Beth bit into a warm croissant. 'He'll be out all day and has left a list of work to be done on the computer.'

Beth couldn't help feeling pleased that she wouldn't have to see her employer for the rest of the day and the relief must have shown on her face for Juanita asked curiously, 'Is everything all right, Beth? How are you finding your new job?'

'Well, it's only been one day, of course, but the job's really interesting,' she said brightly.

'And what about Vincente? He demands a lot, my cousin. Do you think you two will work well together?'

'I hope so. This job means a lot to me, Juanita, and I'm determined to prove myself. In fact, I intend to become indispensable to your cousin!'

Juanita let out a peal of laughter.

'Then, Beth, I wish you the best of luck. I have a feeling that my formidable cousin has no idea what he has let himself in for.'

Over the next few days Beth saw little of her employer as she manned the office single-handed and worked through the tasks that appeared each day on the computer screen. The work was so varied and made such good use of her linguistic skills that she found it completely engrossing and had no qualms about working late to finish each day's work, often missing dinner altogether and having a solitary supper in her room at bedtime.

Juan often asked her out to dine and when she refused he would pull a face and declare that Vincente was a slave driver. Beth always found herself leaping to the defence of her absent boss.

Inwardly, though, she knew Juan had a point. She couldn't continue with the frantic workload she had set herself and was keen to speak to Vincente about a more balanced approach.

Unfortunately he was nowhere to be found. He was out during the day, never appeared in the evenings, and when Beth queried his absence from the dinner table, Juanita merely shrugged her shoulders and said she assumed he was out with Diane.

One night, her mind still buzzing from some work she had just completed, she found herself unable to sleep. After slipping on her robe she tiptoed through the quiet house to the kitchen to make herself a milky drink. She was just pouring the hot milk into a mug when a soft sound alerted her and she whipped round to see Vincente framed in the doorway.

'Goodness!' she exclaimed. 'You gave me quite a fright!'

'Sorry. I didn't mean to startle you. I've just got in and thought I'd make myself some coffee.'

Beth eyed him curiously, wondering why he had forsaken his usual elegant attire for denims and a black T-shirt and, when he moved closer and the strip lighting picked out the dark smudges beneath his eyes, she gave abrupt voice to her thoughts.

'You look quite exhausted!'

A rueful smile crossed his face.

'That's hardly surprising since I've been working a fourteen-hour day for the last week.'

'Look,' she said, gesturing towards the kitchen table, 'you sit down and I'll make the coffee.'

To her surprise he did as she suggested and when she handed over a steaming mug of coffee he breathed in the aroma, drank deeply, then said, 'This is wonderful, thank you.'

He leaned back, dark eyes appraising her.

'And why are you here at this late hour, Beth?'

When she admitted she had been unable to sleep he stifled a yawn.

'Don't mention the word or I'll collapse at this very table.'

She waited for him to go on and, when he didn't, she prompted him.

'Are you going to tell me what you've been doing all week, or is it to remain a secret?'

He gave a great guffaw of laughter.

'I think you're entitled to know. One of the smaller vineyards, a family concern we bought a few years ago, was in danger of grinding to a halt. The original owners stayed on as managers and, unfortunately, some sort of infection has hit the family, preventing them from working all week. Naturally, I stepped in to keep the place going as there was no-one else. I'm pleased to report that the Rodrigues family is well on the way to recovery and everything should be back to normal by next week.'

'I see,' Beth said, although she didn't fully understand why he hadn't asked other family members, notably Juan, to help out.

As though in answer to her unspoken query he went on, 'There was no-one here who could help me, you know. For reasons known only to the twins they have always avoided direct involvement with the vineyards. With no practical experience of wine-growing they would have been a liability. I wasn't snubbing them by not asking for their help, just being practical.'

'You don't have to explain yourself to me,' Beth said stiffly. 'It's none of my business.'

'It's very much your business. You've been holding the fort in my absence and I know you've been considerably overworked.'

'I guess we've both had a hard week,' Beth conceded.

'Well, I can promise you next week will be very different. In the meantime,' he went on with mock solemnity, 'I order you to enjoy your weekend. Do you have any plans?'

'Juanita has suggested we go to one of the local markets.'

'Take her up on that. Boss's orders.'

He rose and stood looking down at her, his face an impenetrable mask.

'I'll say good-night now. And thanks

again for the support you've given me this week.'

She watched his retreating back, a frown crossing her face. She couldn't accuse him of being unappreciative of the long hours she had put in over the last difficult week but it would have been better if he had explained the situation earlier and not left her in the dark. She could only conclude that Vincente was a man who was so used to depending solely on himself that, intentionally or otherwise, he ended up excluding all those around him.

In spite of her late night, Beth found herself feeling remarkably fresh the following morning and, as it was the day of her shopping trip with Juanita, she got up with a keen sense of anticipation. After a light breakfast they set off in Juanita's open-topped car.

'La Fortuna is one of our most beautiful villages,' Juanita enthused. 'It consists principally of one street lined with lovely old houses and on Saturday mornings the market takes over the whole village.'

Beth turned her attention to the scenery. They had left behind the fertile plain of the valley and now the land was opening up into gentle sierras and plateaus. There was little sign of habitation and the road they were travelling on cut straight across the farming land. It was breathtaking and her spirits soared and the cares of her frantic week fell away.

Juanita slowed the car to take a tight corner and as they swung to the right she said, 'La Fortuna is just coming into view.'

Beth looked in delight at the sight of the white buildings with red-tiled roof tops twisting up the hillside. They followed the signs to the designated carpark and, after parking, set off along a footpath which wound up the hillside and led them directly into the alleyway which ran on to the high street. As they joined the crowds jostling for space around the stalls Beth wondered for a moment how she was going to fight her way through the scrum but Juanita showed herself to be an expert at cutting a path through the crowds and Beth followed in her wake, happy to let her lead the way, as she directed her to the stalls where she would find the best bargains.

After an hour, Juanita suggested they break for lunch and they headed into a network of side streets. To Beth's relief it was much cooler down these deserted alleyways where the buildings, shuttered against the fierce midday sun, cast a welcome shade. Juanita stopped abruptly.

'Here we are. Frederico makes the best tapas in the whole region,' and then she disappeared down a flight of steps on her left.

Beth hurriedly followed to find herself in a dimly-lit bar, the floor dotted by small round tables. Juanita greeted a tall, moustachioed man like an old friend. He ushered them to a table, clicking his fingers at a young man leaning against the bar who then strolled over to take their drinks order.

'Perhaps I should be drinking wine,' Beth said, 'now that I'm involved with wine makers.'

'Members of the Perez family haven't actually made any wine for two generations. The managers run the vineyards, Vincente runs the marketing side, and Juan and I have the good fortune to be able to live off the profits.'

How cool she sounded! Taken aback by this attitude Beth remained silent but Juanita, sensing her disapproval, appraised her with narrowed eyes.

'Now I have shocked you! I can see you think that I live a useless, idle sort of life.'

'It really isn't any of my business how you live your life,' Beth said, glad of an interruption when the waiter arrived to hand them their drinks.

'True,' Juanita said as she looked absently down into her wine glass, 'but I wouldn't like you to think I was just a spoiled, little rich girl, Beth. Juan and I grew up to have our hopes and dreams just like any other young people. I was always good at languages and dreamed of working abroad. Juan, well, he has gifts in art and he longed to go to Barcelona and study with the best tutors. We talked endlessly of our plans, but . . . '

Her voice trailed away, her expression clouded, and Beth leaned forward and touched her gently on the arm.

'What happened? Why didn't you realise your dreams?'

'Because they never fitted in with Father's plans for us.'

Her face was a picture of resentment and Beth hardly recognised her.

'We had been brought up to play some sort of rôle in the family business, although neither of us had any real interest in it. We tried to tell Father that but he just wouldn't listen. Juan was put through some course in business studies in Madrid which he absolutely hated and I was sent off to a finishing school in Switzerland. You see, I was supposed to catch the eye of some rich businessman.'

'That sounds as though your father saw you as some sort of commodity!' Beth said, appalled at what she was hearing.

'I am simply stating the facts,' Juanita returned. 'It's no use pretending we had an easy relationship with our father. Our mother died giving birth to us and I often wondered if he held us responsible for the tragedy. We were brought up by nannies and Father remained a cool and remote figure. It's little wonder that we had problems communicating as a family.'

It was a sad story and in some ways paralleled her own life for, separated from her own parents throughout much of her childhood, relations between them had grown increasingly distant. When she relayed her own experience Juanita expressed sympathy.

'Then you know what it feels like.'

'I did have Gran,' Beth pointed out. 'She was always a support.'

'I, too, had support in the form of my

twin. We stood together against the world, Beth, and that made our childhood a lot easier.'

The tray of tapas arrived and as they picked out the tempting delicacies they lapsed into silence, but Beth was curious to know more about the Perez family and, her appetite satisfied, she leaned back.

'I know I'm touching on delicate matters but what was your reaction to Vincente when he first arrived?' she asked.

Juanita seemed happy to answer.

'We gave him a very warm welcome! We had no idea why Father and Uncle Esteban had fallen out but we were happy to meet our cousin for the first time. He was very intriguing to us, you see, as he had lived abroad and done so many of the things we had dreamed of doing. He was a great help, too, when Father was diagnosed with the illness which killed him so quickly. We were on good terms with our cousin, Beth, until we discovered he had stolen our inheritance!'

Now they had come to the crux of the problem.

'When did your father actually change his will?' Beth ventured.

'After he was told about his illness.'

Her face twisted, briefly, with distaste.

'That was several months after Vincente appeared in our lives. He had ample time to worm his way into Father's affections.'

'Aren't you being a little hard on our cousin?' Beth felt impelled to say. 'Is it his fault your father chose to behave in such an irrational manner?'

'He could have done the right thing and refused the inheritance,' Juanita returned bitterly, and Beth found herself in agreement, wondering why Vincente had decided to accept a bequest not rightfully his.

Juanita answered her unspoken query.

'He gave in to greed, Beth. He wanted to fill his own pockets. So we played him at his own game. He knew that if we took legal action we would have dragged his name through the mud, so he settled out of court, to our considerable advantage. Neither Juan nor I will have to worry about money for the rest of our lives!'

In spite of her triumphant tone Beth sensed unhappiness behind her words and ventured a suggestion of her own.

'If that's the case then why don't you and Juan fulfil some of those dreams you had when you were younger?'

'Perhaps, but isn't that just what Vincente would want, for us to leave Casa Perez so that he can lord it around in our absence? I don't feel like making my cousin that happy, Beth.'

Beth had the distinct feeling that this was just an excuse and that Juanita and her brother were in danger of settling into a life which had little purpose in it, motivated only by a desire to make their cousin's life as difficult as possible. Inwardly she reminded herself once more that it was none of her business how the Perez family managed their lives, and that if she was to make a success of her job she must remain detached. She was fully aware, though, that keeping that resolution might well prove difficult.

5

The next morning, after a leisurely breakfast, Beth went down to the swimming pool where she found Juan and Juanita frolicking in the water and Diane stretched out on a sunlounger topping up her tan. Diane raised her eyes at Beth's approach, glanced lazily up and down, and said, 'I hope you have sun tan lotion on, honey, or that skin of yours will surely burn.'

'Actually, I use a complete sun block. I burn easily and don't tan at all.'

'Really?'

Her beautifully-plucked eyebrows arched as though she had never heard of such a thing and then she replaced her sunglasses and stretched languidly. Juanita had watched this exchange with some amusement and when Beth dived in and swam to join her she spoke in a low voice.

'Don't mind Diane. She sees every woman as a potential rival.'

'Well, she can count me out,' Beth snapped. 'I'm hardly in her league!'

'You're far beyond it!'

Juan had crept up, unannounced, his arm snaking around Beth's waist as he challenged her to a race.

Beth accepted, so with Juanita acting as umpire, they set off to do two lengths which ended with a close win for Beth which was disputed, good naturedly, by Juan.

Halfway through the morning, Diane announced that she had a business engagement and would they apologise to Vincente for her as she wouldn't be able to join him for lunch as usual. After she had sauntered off, the twins departed, too, for a pre-arranged visit to friends and Beth was left alone.

After swimming a few more lengths she turned over on her back and floated, her eyes closing and her thoughts wandering as the water rocked her gently from side to side. It occurred to her that she had hardly thought of her errant ex-fiancé since she had joined the household at Casa Perez. It had only been a couple of weeks ago that she had received the letter which had blown her life apart yet, already, Patrick seemed to belong to another world, which had no connection to the one she now inhabited.

Was she so superficial that she was able to forget Patrick as soon as his love for her had grown cold, or was she simply blocking out his memory because his dismissal of her was too much to bear? There was no easy answer, she decided at last, feeling thoroughly confused. Besides, it was fruitless to dwell on the past when her new life at Casa Perez required all her attention. Just keeping on good terms with her new boss as well as maintaining her friendship with the twins would require all the tact and diplomacy she could muster.

Luxuriating in the warmth of the midday sun and the weightlessness of her body she allowed her thoughts to drift and was so successful that she did not hear her name, softly spoken, until it was repeated. Her eyes opened reluctantly and she found herself looking up into Vincente's face. He was standing at the poolside, peering down at her. She flipped herself over, her feet just touching the bottom as she stood up to face him.

He smiled.

'I'm sorry to disturb you, you looked wonderfully peaceful, but I wanted to ask you something.'

'I'll just get out and then we can speak properly.'

She swam to the side, and, as she attempted to lever herself up, he reached down and lifted her out of the water as though she was weightless. As he set her on her feet she found herself within the circle of his arms. She stepped back abruptly.

'I'm wetting you!' she exclaimed.

He scooped up a large towel from the pool surround, handing it to her.

'Thank you,' Beth said, and she began to rub herself down vigorously, all too conscious of the skimpiness of her bikini and of his gaze upon her.

As though aware of her embarrassment, there was a hint of amusement in the depths of his eyes but his voice was businesslike when he spoke.

'I wondered what you were doing for lunch today, Beth. The Rodriguez family has asked me to eat with them to thank me for all the work I've put in at their vineyard this week. As I would never have managed to do that without you keeping the office going in my absence I thought you might like to come, too.'

Beth found herself seeking for an excuse.

'I wouldn't wish to impose myself on the Rodriguez family if they're only expecting one person.'

He flashed her a smile.

'They're not. They asked me to bring a guest.'

Now she understood! Vincente

needed a companion and she was the only woman available as Diane was otherwise engaged!

'It sounds as though it's all been decided,' she couldn't help saying.

'Only to your advantage,' he said breezily. 'Senora Rodriguez is renowned for her cooking and a trip to their place would provide you with a chance to view a perfect example of a traditional vineyard. You'd enjoy it.'

'Give me five minutes to change,' Beth said, realising it would be churlish to refuse.

He strode away from her, throwing his reply over his shoulder.

'I'll hold you to that, Beth. I'll see you at my car.'

Beth hurried to her room, showered, slipped into a crisp, cotton dress in a vivid shade of blue, gave one cursory glance at herself in the mirror, and then hurried out into the sunshine to rejoin Vincente. As she approached he looked meaningfully down at his watch.

'I'm impressed. The women I know

usually keep me waiting far longer,' he said.

As she settled herself into the passenger seat she wondered, fleetingly, just how many women he did know. There was Diane, of course, but although she liked to give the impression at every available opportunity that Vincente was hers for the asking, Beth wasn't quite so sure. Although she had only known her employer a short time she had gained the distinct impression of a strong-willed, independent man unlikely, as yet, to give up his freedom for any woman.

For one, brief moment she found herself in the unusual position of feeling sorry for the American woman who, in spite of her beauty and myriad attractions, seemed to have set her heart on someone destined to elude her. Next moment Vincente punctured her thoughts.

'We have plenty of time to take the scenic route, Beth, so I think we'll take the old coast road out of Alicante.'

As they joined the road which hugged the coastline, Beth gazed upon the sparkling water which mirrored the perfectly blue sky and began to relax, enthralled by the beauty of it all. Vincente kept up a flow of conversation, pointing out sights of interest on the way, and she had to remind herself that he was a relative newcomer to this part of the world.

'Anyone would think you were born and bred here, Vincente, the way you speak with such passion about this land.'

'In a way I was, Beth. Some of my earliest memories are of Father telling me of the beauty of the Alicante region. He painted pictures in my mind that were so vivid that when I came here for the first time there was a comfortable familiarity about the landscape.'

He spoke with so much feeling that Beth was silent a moment and then she returned to a less personal topic.

'How traditional is the vineyard we

are going to, and what type of wine does the Rodriguez family make?'

'It is very traditional,' he said emphatically. 'Look,' he said, waving one hand to his right.

They had just entered wine-making country and the fields were dotted with arched porches which Beth knew were characteristic of the region.

'Those arches,' he added, 'are kept for sentimental reasons by most wine growers but Senor Rodriguez still uses his to dry his grapes. Also, he uses only native varieties for his vines, such as Monastrel, and specialises in Rosés which he makes using a method which goes back generations.'

Beth pulled a face.

'Then how did he feel about being swallowed up by a large concern?'

'Delighted, as it happens. He was on the verge of bankruptcy which meant he would have lost the home the family had lived in for generations as well as his livelihood. By accepting our offer, he was able to retain his home and continue to manage the place as he sees fit.'

Beth shot him a sceptical glance.

'You don't run a charity, Vincente, so what does your company gain?'

He gave a low-throated chuckle.

'We gain specialist wines, made by traditional methods, which attract a healthy premium in the best restaurants.'

He was every inch the businessman, she concluded silently, and without wanting to be disloyal to the twins she could hardly see either of them, with their unworldly ideas and romantic notions, fitting into the niche Vincente filled so effectively.

When they drew up outside the long, low white building, though, and the whole of the Rodriguez family came out to greet them, three generations of smiling, chattering people who treated them as though they were long lost friends, Beth could only applaud Vincente's actions. Senor Rodriguez insisted on taking her around, proudly showing her the vats where the first light crushing of the grapes took place and explaining everything in detail. He spoke rapidly, in such a strong regional accent, that Beth had some difficulty in understanding him. She found it best just to nod and smile and hope that he would be happy with her response.

Soon the senora called them to come and eat and they joined the rest of the family at the long table set in the shade of an ancient oak where the numbers seemed to have been swelled by neighbours. Beth was introduced to a bewildering number of people, whose names she knew she would never remember. But a handshake and a warm smile seemed all that was required to form a bond and she sat back and prepared to enjoy herself, as the food appeared and the wine flowed. It became obvious, after a while, that they were under the misapprehension that she was Vincente's date and when she tried to make them see otherwise, her cheeks scarlet, she was met with sceptical looks and even broader grins.

Looking across at Vincente for help she not only found him avoiding her eyes but accepting the congratulations of the men at having found himself such a beautiful girl, with a careless shrug of his shoulders. Later, after they had said their farewells and were walking towards the car, Beth asked him why he had joined in so readily with the charade.

'I was just being polite, Beth, that's all. It was just innocent fun.'

He paused in the process of opening the passenger door for her.

'Surely you don't object?'

'No, of course not,' she said hastily, not wanting to appear too prim. 'Besides,' she added, as she fastened her seat belt, 'as I can barely follow the local dialect, most of the time I didn't know what they were saying.'

'Well, as some of the men were, shall we say, rather fulsome in their praise of you, perhaps that's just as well,' Vincente offered, smiling.

Back at Casa Perez she found that the twins had returned and wanted to know all about her day. After she had told them of her visit to the Rodriguez family with Vincente, Juan made a show of mock jealousy and insisted that she should accept a dinner invitation from him in the week to make up for her fickle behaviour with his cousin.

'Why not?' she said easily.

Juan was fun to be with and she felt pretty confident that she would be able to enjoy his company without the risk of encouraging attentions which she was not yet ready to meet. They decided on an evening mid-week, Beth adding the proviso, work permitting, but in the event, she had no problem in meeting her obligation. Now that Vincente was back in the office the workload was much lighter. He was on hand to answer any queries she might have, and, to her surprise, she found that they slotted effortlessly into working as a team.

The light was fading as she and Juan

drew to a halt in front of a
set on the jetty of a sma
which, according to Juan,
finest seafood menu on the
warm enough to eat outside so they
settled themselves on the terrace, lit by
fairy lights, which overlooked the dark
ocean. With Juan's help she chose from
the menu and, whilst they ate, he
amused her with stories of his time in
England at various language schools
and of his highly-inventive ways of
avoiding lessons in order to pursue a
wilder teenage life.

'I think I would have been thrown
out on many occasions if not for my
sister. Juanita was such a model pupil I
think they were afraid that, if I went,
she'd follow.'

'She's certainly keen on the language.
She told me that she thought of
working in an English-speaking country.'

'Well, that was not to be. Father had
other plans for us. It's a great pity that,
whilst he was busy messing up our lives

e sake of the family business, he
n't tell us that he was going to
isinherit us in favour of a relative who
would turn up out of the blue one day.'

Shocked by the bitterness in his tone
she reached forward to cover his hand
with hers as he went on.

'It would be easier to bear if I knew
for certain he really was our cousin.'

'Surely you're not suggesting that
Vincente is some sort of impostor?'

'No, not in the sense you mean. It's
just that, well . . . '

As though he had mentally shaken
himself he went on more coherently.

'You see, there are people who
remember Vincente's mother, Victoria.
Carla, our housekeeper for one. Victoria
came to the area as an au pair and, as
she was very beautiful, she was pursued
by a number of young men. Apparently
Uncle Esteban was not one of them.'

Perplexed, Beth, said, 'So?'

'Well, Victoria went home to England
all of a sudden, and there was gossip.
Uncle Esteban followed in due course

but it was some time before they married. It was believed here that he'd married her to help her out of an unfortunate situation.'

'So, you're suggesting that Vincente was not your uncle's son?'

'I'm just repeating local gossip, Beth, only the situation's even harder to bear if Vincente is not a blood relative after all.'

'Juan, you have nothing to go on but rumours and innuendo!'

'That doesn't mean it's not true!'

Beth held up her hands.

'Juan, I don't want to hear any more of this! I know you've a grievance against Vincente but please remember he is my employer. I really don't think it's right for me to be discussing his mother's personal private life.'

At this, Juan looked shamefaced.

'You're right. I shouldn't be involving you in all this. I'm sorry, Beth, I won't do it again.'

Beth didn't doubt his sincerity but she also doubted that he'd stick to his resolution. Bitterness towards Vincente was eating away at him.

Hoping to get on to a more positive topic Beth said, 'Juanita said you're a really fine artist. What sort of work do you specialise in?'

He shrugged his shoulders.

'I only daub a little.'

'That's not what I heard. Come on,' she coaxed. 'I'd love to hear about your painting. Do you paint portraits or scenery?'

'Landscapes,' Juan said, with sudden animation, 'local scenes, mostly, in water colours. In my teens I experimented with a lot of bold colour but in the last few years I've settled on a quieter style. In Spain we live with strong colour every day so, in my work, I try to tone that down by using water colours. It allows for more subtlety.'

'And what about further study? Juanita said it was your ambition, at one time, to study in Barcelona.'

'Well, that was another plan Father ruined. It didn't fit in with his idea of me as an international businessman but by the time he realised I'd never make the grade in that sort of life it was too late.'

'But you're a free agent, now,' Beth pointed out. 'Surely it's time to follow your dream.'

His expression clouded.

'But that's all it ever was, Beth, a young man's dream. I realise that now. That's something Father did bequeath to me, a sense of reality.'

Beth felt sudden anger for the way in which the late Felipe Perez had sapped his children's ambitions in an attempt to mould them to his will, only to reject them cruelly at the end of his life. But raking over the past would not help Juan now.

'Would you let me see some of your work?' she asked kindly.

'Do you really wish to see my childish efforts?'

'I do,' she confirmed.

'Then I'll show them to you, as long as you promise not to laugh!'

As they laughed together the atmosphere lightened, and when Juan suggested they go on to a night club Beth was happy to comply as she, too, felt that it was far too early to go home. They ended up in a small club that Beth knew well in Puerto del Segura and she and Juan took the floor, relishing the chance to enjoy the music.

Later, the music changed to a slower beat and the floor was crowded with couples entwined in each other's arms. Juan drew her into his arms but she felt a tension rising within her. We're only dancing, she reminded herself, trying to relax, but another part of her mind was telling her that it was far too soon after Patrick to be thinking of another relationship. She knew, with a woman's instinct, that Juan was very attracted to her, and, at some point, she would have to be completely honest and tell him she was not seeking romance, although she did want to retain his friendship.

She was to face her problem sooner than she expected for, as the music came to a halt, Juan swung her round deftly and, before she realised what was happening, she had been manoeuvred on to the terrace where they found themselves alone. Juan's eyes were as dark as the night sky as he looked down at her.

'Beth, you are so beautiful.'

His lips moved across hers but Beth's immediate response was to tense and draw back. As he looked down at her, disappointment written across his handsome features, Beth felt terrible but she knew she finally had to clear the air between them.

'I'm sorry,' she whispered, 'but we really need to talk.'

She took his hand in hers and led him to the parapet which overlooked a spectacular view over the moonlit ocean. She turned to face him.

'There's no easy way to say this but the fact is I've just come out of a broken engagement. I was jilted in a very cruel manner and I feel far too bruised to even think of another involvement. I'm just not ready, Juan.'

He was silent a moment but, when he spoke, his concern was evident.

'This man must have hurt you very much, Beth. And he must be very foolish to give up such a prize!'

Beth couldn't help smiling.

'That's what I tell myself. But, seriously, I really do value your company and your friendship. I don't want this to spoil things between us.'

'Oh, it won't,' he said emphatically. 'I notice you say you are not ready yet. Does that mean that there might be some hope for me in the future?'

Beth's blue eyes twinkled up at him.

'There's always hope, Juan.'

'Then, that, dearest Beth, is good enough for me,' he said, kissing her softly on the forehead.

They left soon after and, although Juan was a little subdued, Beth felt that their friendship hadn't been seriously damaged by their frank talk. As they drew up to the house she had a sudden idea.

'Juan, why don't you show me some of your paintings now?'

He gave her a mischievous smile.

'Why, Beth, what are you suggesting? I keep them in my room. It could ruin your reputation.'

'I'm sure my reputation will stand it,' she said forthrightly, slipping out of the passenger seat.

Half an hour later, Beth was sitting on the floor in Juan's room surrounded by paintings, some framed and some not. She picked up one of her favourites, a local scene whose subtle blues and violets completely captured its delicate hues, and scanned it once more.

'These really are exquisite, you know,' she said.

Juan, who was sitting on the coffee table facing her, inclined his head.

'Thank you. That means a lot to me.'

She'd no doubt of it. Apart from Juanita, it was unlikely that anyone else had even seen his work. She made a sudden resolution to try and get him to foster his talent but, as a glance at her watch showed her, that must be for another day. It was now very late and it was time for her to go. He showed her out and, after stepping out into the corridor, on impulse, she took his face between her hands and kissed him lightly on the lips.

He reached for her and, laughing, she evaded his grasp but, as she turned away, she found herself facing two figures, standing in the darkness of the corridor, watching curiously. Regaining her composure quickly she raised her head high as she walked past.

'Good-night, Vincente, Diane,' she said wickedly.

Diane shot her an amused glance as she replied but Vincente remained still and silent, his expression dark. She wondered, momentarily, what his cool demeanour meant. Had he misconstrued what he had just seen and was he showing his disapproval? If so he was an arch hypocrite, she decided angrily, for there he was, in Diane's company.

By the time she had reached her room and settled herself into bed she had worked herself up into such a state of indignation that she found it difficult to sleep, the image of Vincente's face, cold and forbidding, haunting her mind until the early hours.

6

To her relief, Vincente said nothing of their night encounter the next day, his manner towards her as professional as ever, and the following week passed uneventfully. As Beth was becoming more used to her varied work schedule she grew in confidence and as queries came in by phone or fax she found that she was increasingly able to deal with them herself without having to consult Vincente.

On the Friday afternoon she was pleased when Vincente suggested she clear her desk and finish work early for the week as she had got through an astounding amount of work and earned some time off. His praise was still ringing in her ears when she met up with Kirsty for an early evening meal in Puerto del Segura and that must have coloured her description of her new job for when she had finished relaying her news Kirsty gazed at her.

'You seem to get on very well with your new boss, Beth,' she concluded.

'We work well as a team and I must say that surprises me,' she admitted. 'When I was first appointed by Vincente I was a little in awe of him. It was quite clear that he was a formidable businessman and that his standards would be exacting. As the job was going to be demanding, I knew it would be a challenge to my skills and, I don't mind admitting, I doubted at times as to whether I'd cope. Now that I've settled in I find the work really interesting and I'm quite at ease with Vincente, in the office, at least.'

'And out of the office?' Kirsty queried.

'Outside work I still find him formidable!' Beth confirmed with a smile. 'So I leave him to the tender mercies of his girlfriend, Diane, and spend most of my time with the twins.'

She went on to talk of them and their

troubled relations with their cousin until Kirsty held up one hand in mock surrender.

'Stop! My head's spinning! It all sounds so complicated.'

'It is, and what it amounts to is that relations are fraught at Casa Perez.'

'Don't get involved,' Kirsty warned. 'It isn't any of your business.'

'I've often told myself the very same thing but it's not as though I'm involved in a nine-to-five job, Kirsty. I live at Casa Perez, I'm part of these people's lives, so it's difficult to remain detached.'

Kirsty appraised her friend, head to one side.

'In that case, I think my warning may have come too late!'

Halfway through the next week, Vincente surprised her one morning when they had stopped for coffee.

'How would you like to come to Barcelona with me, Beth?'

Her face must have looked a picture for he went on quickly.

'I'm talking of a business trip, of course.'

'Naturally, I'll come if I'm needed,' she replied.

'Good, only I think you may be of particular help to me as I shall be meeting with the representative of a British chain of supermarkets who, hopefully, will agree to stock our wine in his stores. His wife will be with him and whilst I talk business with her husband it would be helpful if you could entertain her. I know that isn't strictly within the terms of your job description but I hope you don't object.'

'I've never had a job description,' she couldn't help pointing out, 'and you did warn me that I would need to be flexible. To be frank, it sounds like a dream assignment to me!'

Juanita echoed her sentiments when she told her of the proposed trip after dinner that evening. The two girls were alone and Juanita made no secret of her envy.

'I wish I were going with you, Beth. Barcelona is such an exciting city and the shops are divine! We could have had a wonderful time.'

'It's not only famous for shopping, is it? It's world renowned for its art and architecture. Isn't that where Juan hoped to study?'

'Yes. What, exactly, are you trying to say, Beth?'

'I'm not terribly sure, but ever since I saw Juan's paintings and realised how talented he is I've wanted to do something to encourage him.'

'Well, he certainly won't listen to me on the subject. Just a moment, though. He had an art tutor when he was a teenager who came from Barcelona and when he went back there to work he and Juan kept in touch for a while. It's quite possible his details are still in our address book.'

Getting her drift, Beth suggested, 'So, you'd like me to talk to him and see if he can help Juan in any way.'

'Better still,' Juanita suggested eagerly,

'why don't you take some of Juan's paintings with you? I could smuggle some examples of recent work out of his room and I'm sure we'll be able to return them before he notices they're missing. When Senor Salzillo left the area, Juan was producing good, but immature work. I think he'd be surprised at what he was capable of now.'

It seemed like a marvellous plan and they decided to put it into operation whenever the trip to Barcelona took place. Owing to delays in the schedule of Mr Tennant, the man Vincente was due to meet, the trip didn't take place until the end of the following week but, when they were finally ready to leave, Beth had several pieces of Juan's work hidden away in her suitcase.

One of Vincente's drivers was to take them to Barcelona and throughout the journey Beth sat in the back with her boss as he briefed her on what would be happening during their stay.

'We are due to meet James Tennant

mid-morning for coffee and proceed straight to preliminary talks. I'll need you on hand to furnish all the details I've just been through with you and when we break for lunch Mrs Tennant is expected to join us. In the afternoon her husband and I will get down to some hard bargaining and I will be grateful if you could entertain Mrs Tennant. Then we will all meet up for dinner after what, I hope, will have been a most productive day.'

James Tennant was awaiting them in the lounge of the Hotel Mariola, as expected, and he rose on their approach, hand outstretched. He was a tall man, with thinning brown hair and keen grey eyes which hinted at shrewdness. He seemed surprised to find that Vincente's assistant was a compatriot but confessed that his wife would be very pleased to meet Beth when she joined them later as she spoke no Spanish and was finding herself rather isolated on the trip.

Pleasantries over, they got down to

business and Beth had to keep her wits about her to make sure she did not disrupt the smooth running of Vincente's talk extolling the virtues of Perez vineyards. James Tennant listened intently but when he did ask questions they were to the point, and demonstrated his sure grasp of the issues.

After two hours, they broke for lunch and Beth was now able to meet Sheila Tennant, who turned out to be a pleasant-faced, middle-aged woman who, clearly, loved to talk about her family and, soon, she and Beth were huddled over photographs of her grown-up children and her one grandchild. It became apparent that, now the children were grown up, she felt it her duty to accompany her husband on his buying trips abroad and, equally apparent that she did not enjoy these trips at all.

Lacking other languages she seemed to spend most of her time, when her husband was occupied with business matters, in solitary occupation of her hotel room. She seemed to have seen little of the sights of Barcelona and when Beth offered to show her some she confessed that she had always longed to see the Gaudi cathedral.

'It looks so wonderful in photographs, my dear, quite magical.'

'No photograph can compare with the real thing,' Beth declared, 'so let's leave the men to continue their business and go and see one of the most beautiful buildings in the world.'

Beth was quite familiar with Barcelona and reasonably knowledgeable about Gaudi architecture so when Vincente's driver dropped them at the cathedral she was able to tell Sheila something about the extraordinary building project which had started so many years before. Any gaps in Beth's knowledge were filled in by the guidebooks which were readily available at local kiosks and as they wandered, and wondered, at the unique architectural features of the building Mrs Tennant was clearly awestruck.

'You were so right, my dear,' she commented later when they had stopped for coffee at a little pavement café. 'No photograph can compare with the reality. Thank you so much for being my guide this afternoon.'

Soon afterwards, they took a taxi back to the hotel and, after Beth had escorted a tired but happy Mrs Tennant to her own room, she sped along the corridor, one eye fixed anxiously on her watch. There wasn't much time before she would have to start dressing for dinner so now really was the best time to try to contact Senor Salzillo. Inside her own room she picked up the phone and punched out the number Juanita had given her.

Please be in, she said to herself, as the phone rang and rang. Just as she was about to give up, a male voice answered and when her query confirmed that it was Senor Salzillo speaking she launched into her explanation and request in breathless Spanish.

After she'd finished speaking there

was a pause and then the senor told her that he remembered Juan well and had often wondered what had happened to his old pupil. After a further pause he said that he would love to look at some of Juan's recent work if they could arrange a suitable time and when Beth explained that she would only be in Barcelona for a day or two they fixed on the next afternoon. Hoping that she would be able to slip away from her duties for a couple of hours, Beth scribbled down his address, thanked him, rang off, then whirled off to dress for dinner.

Vincente had arranged for them to eat in the hotel dining-room, which had a good reputation, and, as she hurried to their table, she found everyone else already seated. Vincente rose to pull out her chair for her.

'You look very beautiful tonight, Beth,' he said softly, bringing a flush to her cheeks.

She certainly had tried to make the best of her appearance as she knew that she, as well as Vincente, was representing the Perez business.

Looking across at Mrs Tennant, who was smiling as she read the varied menu, she felt grateful that her first venture into corporate hospitality had brought her into contact with such a pleasant, unassuming woman and not the sort of worldly-wise, business wife she had been expecting.

It was Mrs Tennant who broke the ice by praising Beth for her skills as a guide and, when she and the Tennants realised they had grown up in the same part of London, the conversation flowed. It continued over coffee in the lounge after dinner and when the Tennants rose to go to their rooms Beth and Mrs Tennant agreed to continue their sightseeing the following morning as the men still had business to discuss. When the lift doors closed on their guests, Vincente turned to Beth with a smile.

'Well done, Beth. You've made a hit with Mrs Tennant.'

'She's such a nice person, it's not difficult to get along with her.'

'Even so, you struck up a rapport right away. You've been a real asset.'

His dark eyes smiled into hers and Beth found herself feeling unexpectedly flustered. In an attempt to steer his attentions elsewhere she asked about his business negotiations and her ploy worked so well that he spent the rest of the time they were together filling her in on his progress. One subject Beth did not raise was her proposed visit to Senor Salzillo as she regarded her mission on Juan's account as a personal matter and nothing to do with her work for Vincente. In fact, it was just as well for him to know nothing of her desire to help his cousin.

The following morning Sheila Tennant expressed a wish to shop for gifts and Beth steered her in the direction of one of the local craft makers where she helped her purchase examples of the hand-made ceramics which had taken her eye. Pleased, Sheila Tennant insisted on buying her a selection box of nougat, as a thank you present, and then on taking her to lunch in one of the smart bars that Barcelona was renowned for. By the time they were on to coffee Beth found herself glancing surreptitiously at her watch, conscious that the time of her appointment with Senor Salzillo was close.

Scouring her mind for a suitable excuse for their immediate departure she was pre-empted by Mrs Tennant who, stifling a yawn, expressed a desire to return to the hotel for a siesta. Beth managed to flag down a cab fairly quickly and, after leaving Sheila Tennant in the hotel lobby with a promise to meet up later, she sped up to her room, collected Julian's portfolio then went outside again to ask the doorman to call her a cab.

About ten minutes later, she was climbing out of the taxi in front of the building which housed the senor's apartment. A glance at the names next to the intercom showed that he was on the second floor and, after buzzing him, the heavily-panelled door whirred open and she was drawn into a musty-smelling hallway with a marbled floor and walls in cream.

The clattering of her heels on the stairs must have alerted him for he was waiting for her at his open door, a frail-looking man with a shock of white hair, but there was firmness in his handshake and, after greeting her in Spanish, he switched to accurate but heavily-accented English as he invited her into his lounge. At his behest she seated herself. After she had said yes to refreshments she was surprised to see him bringing in a tea tray.

At her raised brows, he said, 'I taught art in a London college, senorita, many years ago now. I learned there my English, and how to make good tea. And still, senorita, I like to take tea in the afternoon.'

She complimented the senor on his skills as she drank the refreshing liquid and accepted one of the Spanish sweets on offer but she was conscious of the limited time she had, and came to the purpose of her visit.

'I really am grateful, senor, for your offer to look at some of Juan's work. As I explained briefly on the phone yesterday he has virtually stopped painting altogether and his sister is at a loss as to how to proceed. Some encouragement from you might be just what he needs.'

'Juan Perez was a fine student. How I begged his father to send him on to further study, but, no, it was not to be. And now, let me see what the young man is doing now, senorita.'

Beth handed over the portfolio which he took to the table. Switching on a table lamp he spread out Juan's paintings, and began to peer closely at them, muttering to himself in Spanish. Beth watched anxiously, her instincts telling her that the next few moments could be crucial to Juan's future. At last he sat back.

'My old pupil has not developed in

the way I expected, senorita.'

'Does that mean you are disappointed with him?'

His eyes crinkled up as his face broke into a smile.

'Not at all. He is even better than I would have hoped.'

Beth felt relief washing over her.

'Oh, senor, I am so pleased to hear that. Do you think you can help him in any way?'

'Perhaps,' was the succinct reply. 'Much will depend on him. He has talent, you see, but he must work and study. I work some hours at a very good college here. If Juan comes to see me I could introduce him to the principal. Together, perhaps, we can persuade him to study with us.'

'That sounds like a wonderful idea!'

'Talk to him, senorita. Tell him what his old teacher has told you.'

'Certainly, I will,' Beth said as she rose to take her leave, 'and thank you very much for your help.'

Her spirits high, she returned to the

hotel only to bump into Vincente in the lobby.

'You've just missed the Tennants by a whisker,' he told her. 'They've only just checked out.'

Beth expressed her regret.

'Don't worry. You'll be seeing them next week when we take them on a personal tour of our vineyards.'

The delight in his voice was unmistakable and when Beth threw him a quizzical glance he responded with, 'We've done it, Beth! James Tennant seems very satisfied with the product and the prices I'm offering. When we get back to Casa Perez we're to put everything down on paper and fax it to his head office. Assuming they give the green light, and I have no reason to think there'll be a problem. James Tennant will sign the contract when he visits us at Casa Perez!'

Blue eyes shining, Beth looked up at him.

'Vincente, that's wonderful!'

He was very still a moment, then he

131

said, 'I think we deserve a night out, Beth, to celebrate. Barcelona is full of superb restaurants, so let me take you out to supper.'

'I'd like that,' she said, a little shyly.

They arranged to meet later and Beth was left wondering what she ought to wear for a night out with the boss. Vincente had made it clear that they were to forget about work for the night so, in the end, feeling a little reckless, she opted for one of the wilder creations which she had borrowed from Juanita. Strapless, and in a scarlet, silky material which hugged the figure like a second skin, it then flared out, flamenco style, into chiffon below the knee. Beth knew it was suited to her dark colouring.

When she was finally ready, she looked at herself in the cheval mirror and had a sudden attack of nerves. Wouldn't she be better dressed in one of the more conventional outfits she had brought? Wouldn't her appearance be too wild for the fastidious Vincente?

As doubts assailed her once more, she decided to change into the dress she had worn the previous evening but, as her fingers sought for the zip, a knock at the door made her jump. Realising it was now too late to change she picked up her clutch bag and hurried to open the door. Vincente was standing in the corridor with his back to her. He swung round.

'Ah, Beth, I thought we'd . . . '

His voice trailed away as his eyes drank in her appearance.

'Beth, you look quite enchanting,' he said at last.

He drew her arm through his and they set off, Beth with head held high.

7

The bistro which Vincente had chosen was only a short walk away and was very different from the sedate hotel restaurant where they had eaten the previous evening. A hand under her elbow, Vincente shepherded her to a table in the corner, then motioned for the waiter to bring them menus.

'This place seems to be very popular,' she remarked.

'It is. People enjoy the food and then move upstairs to where there's dancing. Perhaps we can do that later.'

Beth swallowed hard before giving a non-committal reply, feeling again that unaccountable tension that Vincente's presence so often wrought in her. In a bid to change her mood she poured herself a large glass of the wine recommended by Vincente, gave verbal approval to his choice, then downed the whole glass. Surprise flashed across his face.

'What on earth are you doing, Beth? Usually you drink very sparingly.'

Beth was now regretting her rash decision to drink on an empty stomach, especially as she was now experiencing a light-headed feeling, but she defended herself by saying, 'I'm simply enjoying the wine.'

'Throwing a fine wine down as though it's pop isn't the way to do it. Or is an attempt to relax? You always seem to be jumpy when I'm around.'

'You're deducing an awful lot from one glass of wine,' she retorted, wondering, suddenly, how they had got into this verbal skirmish.

'Just making an observation, Beth. You're fine with me in the office but outside working hours you avoid me like the plague, preferring the company of my cousins, especially Juan.'

'Vincente, we've touched upon this before. If you're worried about my loyalty I can assure you I do not discuss your business affairs with your relatives, or anyone else for that matter.'

'I know that! I realised very quickly that you were an honest and reliable employee. I'm not calling into question your integrity, I'd just like to know why you're attracted to an empty-headed young man who does nothing with his life but fritter away the money other people earn for him.'

Beth stared at him aghast, acid etching every word of her reply.

'Firstly, I dispute your assessment of your cousin's character, which is coloured by your unfortunate family dispute and, secondly, whom I choose to spend my free time with is none of your business! You didn't buy up my life when you took me on as your assistant!'

Beth was in no mood to worry about the boldness of her response. Vincente had infuriated her by his arrogant intrusion into her private affairs and she was not prepared to give way. A waiter appeared at her elbow but, as she turned and he caught sight of her expression, he backed away.

'There's no need to take it out on the hapless waiter, Beth. Save your anger for me.'

He took the full impact of her fierce, blue eyes.

'I shall be delighted to.'

He raised his hands in mock surrender.

'Look, I'm sorry I've upset you by commenting on your private life. I don't know how we got into this squabble but I'm sure it was all my fault.'

'It was,' Beth told him bluntly.

She had been on the point of walking out but an apology from a man who, normally, never showed any humility had thrown her, especially when he covered her hand with his and asked her to forgive his stupid behaviour and stay. Breathlessly she found herself agreeing, although she had doubts as to whether the evening could be salvaged.

In that she was wrong. When the food

eventually arrived it was delicious and Vincente, in another characteristic change of mood, began a lively and amusing discourse on the differences between English and Spanish customs. Later, laughing at one of his jokes as they finished their dessert, it was hard to believe that the evening had begun on such a sour note. When he suggested they join the dancers upstairs, Beth was happy to comply.

Beth enjoyed dancing and they managed to find a space on the crowded dance floor which allowed enough room for her to give full rein to her natural sense of rhythm. Vincente, his jacket removed, displayed all the natural grace she would have expected of such an elegant man and more than one admiring eye was drawn to the handsome couple. After one particularly energetic dance Beth swung round with a flourish, laughter spilling from her lips, to find herself held in an embrace and Vincente's eyes looking into hers.

'The music has slowed,' he murmured.

The music may have slowed but her heart appeared to have speeded up! He drew her closer so that her cheek was against the silkiness of his shirt. They moved as though they were one and Vincente's closeness began to weave a spell which threatened to breach the defences she had built up around herself since she had received Patrick's heartless letter.

The music stopped and Beth was stepping out of Vincente's arms when, without a word, he took hold of her hand and led her from the floor towards a door which led them up a flight of stairs and on to a roof terrace. She followed without protest as though she was in a dream and then found herself in a truly magical place. Small lemon and orange trees in dark green containers were dotted about the decked flooring and the full length of the parapet was lined by planters from which brightly-coloured flowers sprang.

Crossing to the parapet Beth looked over to find herself staring down at a small square, which obviously served as a communal garden, with benches and neat flower beds cut into the paving, a decorative, cast iron lamppost casting a rosy glow. Only the faint thrum of traffic in the distance gave any hint that they were in the centre of Barcelona.

'What a lovely place,' she breathed, 'like a secret hideaway.'

Vincente was beside her and one hand stroked up her arm as he turned her to face him.

'Perhaps it is a place where we can dream a little, Beth.'

His hand cradled the back of her head as he raised her face to meet his lips. For one entrancing moment time hung still and then Beth was responding to him with an urgency which, if she had been in full control of her senses, she would have found shocking. After what seemed like an age his lips broke from hers.

'I've tried so hard not to give in to

what I feel for you, Beth, but when I saw you tonight my resistance crumbled,' he whispered.

Beth could barely take in what he was saying and, what was more, barely cared, wanting only his lips to return to hers. She reached up to cradle his face in her hands, the message in her eyes unmistakeable, and he dipped his head once more to draw her into a kiss which sent her senses reeling.

Suddenly the door burst open spilling a group of laughing, chattering youngsters on to the roof terrace. Plucked from the magic of Vincente's arms Beth was hardly aware of her surroundings and, afterwards, she could recall little of their silent walk back to the hotel, hand in hand. When they reached her room she looked up at Vincente, ready to speak, but he laid one gentle finger on her lips.

'No. We will talk in the morning. Good-night, dearest Beth.'

His lips brushed her brow and then he was gone.

Beth slept surprisingly well and the next morning she awoke, immediately alert, her mind full of what had happened between her and Vincente. In the cold light of day her behaviour of the previous evening seemed foolish, if not downright reckless. He was already involved with Diane and, even if he were not, any sort of relationship between them was out of the question. After her recent break up with Patrick she had constantly told herself that she must not consider another romance too soon.

An unbidden memory of the eager way in which she had responded to Vincente stole into her mind and she forced herself to contrast that with the way in which she had brushed off Juan's attempt to get close. Why had she been so inconsistent? Especially when she knew that she liked, and trusted Juan. As for Vincente, she had no real inkling as to her feelings for him.

Up until the first stirrings of

attraction last night she had never, for one moment, considered that there could ever be anything between them. No-one could deny that he was a very attractive man but he was a complete mystery to her, and, she felt sure, far beyond her reach. Diane, the glamorous Californian, was a much more suitable match for him, and any attempt on her part to rival her would surely come to grief. Her heart had been broken, all too recently, when she had allowed herself to fall in love with her boss. She would be a fool, indeed, to repeat the same mistake.

She rose, slipped on her robe, and began to pace about restlessly, wondering how to resolve the awkward situation between herself and Vincente. Of course she had no idea how he viewed what had happened last night. It might have been a mere flirtation. The air must be cleared between them if they were to go on working together. She tried to marshal her thoughts as to the best way to tackle such a delicate subject but kept on drawing a blank.

She swung round at a knock on the door and had barely called out permission to enter when Vincente stepped into the room carrying a breakfast tray. He unloaded it on to the low table and straightened.

'As you didn't come down to breakfast I've brought you up some coffee and croissants.'

He caught sight of her troubled expression.

'What's the matter, Beth? Is there something wrong,' he added.

How cool and composed he appeared, whilst she was in such a state of turmoil she had been unable to dress, unable to even think! Resentment welled up within her at the way in which he seemed able to cut off from his emotions and her tone was quite brusque when she spoke.

'I think we must clear the air about what happened last night. Of course, I was as much to blame as you.'

'Oh, were you?'

Hands on hips, he surveyed her, scepticism etched into every word.

'Why are you apportioning blame, Beth? What was so terrible about what happened between us?'

Beth tried again, inwardly willing herself to come up with the right words.

'It wasn't terrible, but it certainly was a mistake.'

'In what way?'

'In every way. We work together and we should keep our relationship totally professional. Besides,' she went on frantically, 'there are commitments elsewhere.'

Did she have to spell it out to him? Had he forgotten Diane?

'Oh, I see, commitments,' he repeated meaningfully. 'Now we come to the real reason you're freezing me out. Well, I won't make a nuisance of myself, Beth.'

He turned to go and, in sudden realisation that she had handled matters clumsily, Beth called him back.

'Wait, Vincente, don't go, please. I'm

sorry I sounded so harsh just now. I simply wanted to straighten things out between us. I really don't want this to spoil the working relationship we've built up.'

His expression was bleak as he looked at her.

'Don't worry, Beth. I'm not vindictive enough to take this out on you professionally. In that area of my life, at least, you have made yourself quite indispensable.'

If not in other areas, was the unspoken message, and, after he had left Beth found herself staring, unseeing, at the closed door, wondering how she had managed to make quite such a mess of things.

Once they returned to Casa Perez, Beth was so busy with the paper work pertaining to the Tennant deal she had little time to brood on her complicated personal life. At least as far as Juan's artistic future was concerned Beth would report a positive outcome to his sister, and after listening carefully to

Beth's report Juanita clapped her hands in glee.

'Oh, I knew you would bring us luck, Beth. I felt it as soon as we met you! This might be just the thing to motivate Juan.'

Beth urged caution.

'I hope so, but we've yet to persuade Juan to act on it and he might be very angry that we went behind his back.'

'That is true. But, Beth, we have no choice but to be frank with him. We must tell him what we did and then we must take the consequences.'

Juan was surprised that evening when his sister and Beth declared that they were taking him out to dinner and, when they met Vincente and Diane in the hallway on the way out, he joked, one arm placed possessively around Beth, that he was being kidnapped by two beautiful women.

'How very fortunate for you,' Vincente remarked, his eyes averted from Beth's whilst Diane barely acknowledged their presence.

Vincente was dressed in a dinner suit, Diane matching him for style in a full-length gown in black velvet, daringly slit up to the right thigh, and Beth wondered, fleetingly, where they were going. Juan enlightened her as they went out to his car.

'My dear cousin and his lady friend are going to a business dinner tonight. I am sure it will be full of people talking about nothing but winemaking and will be desperately dull. How pleased I am not to be with them. I had much rather be with my favourite English girl.'

He squeezed Beth around the waist and Beth wondered if he would be so pleased with her when he discovered the real purpose of their outing.

★ ★ ★

'You did what?'

Juanita leaned across the restaurant table to whisper warningly.

'Lower your voice, Juan. We don't want everyone to know your business.'

'I can hardly stay calm,' Juan hissed back, 'not after what you two have just told me.'

Beth watched in dismay as Juan switched to Spanish, his angry words and his sister's retort spoken so rapidly that Beth had little chance of following. Juan's furious demeanour needed little interpretation, however, and Beth waited apprehensively for his angry tirade to be over. At last he lapsed into silence and, in answer to Beth's enquiring look, Juanita spoke.

'My brother believes we have betrayed him, Beth.'

Beth found herself the focus of Juan's accusing eyes as he spoke.

'I thought you were my friend. I did not think you would deceive me.'

'I am your friend. That's why I did what I did. Can't you see that? I used some subterfuge and I'm sorry for that but I genuinely had your best interests at heart.'

She could see that Juan was a little mollified by her plea and she pressed on a little further.

'And it was worth the effort, Juan. Senor Salzillo was really impressed by your work. He made it clear that he had always thought you had talent but your progress has been even better than expected. He believes that, with study, you could really make a mark in the art world and he's willing to help you take those first steps. What do you say?'

'I say you have a silver tongue, Beth. I can see that you two thought you were helping me but I still think it's up to me to decide how to run my life.'

'Of course,' Juanita said, 'but surely, as your twin, I can help it along in the right direction.'

Juan looked back at Beth, eyes heavenward.

'Never have I won an argument with my sister. Do you think I ever will?'

'Probably not.'

Beth smiled, relieved that his good humour was restored. Later, when he was away paying the bill she discussed his reaction with Juanita.

'Don't be too worried about his anger,' Juanita said. 'Juan soon loses his temper but he is just as quick to calm down. We've hurt his pride a little by going behind his back but when he's had a chance to think it all over, he'll realise we're offering him an opportunity to change his life for the better. You've done your part, Beth, now it's up to me to keep up the pressure on him. I won't let him forget what Senor Salzillo said about his work.'

'I just hope things work out for him.'

'I hope so, too. It's about time one of us had some purpose in life.'

The next few days were spent on finalising details for the visit of the Tennants and Beth was relieved to find that Vincente was out of the office for much of the time, making the task much easier. In spite of her best efforts, the atmosphere between them was still strained.

She was mulling this over mid-morning when the door burst open and Vincente strode in, his expression as dark as a storm-tossed day.

'What on earth's happened?' Beth asked.

'You may well ask! I've just had a very awkward conversation with James Tennant. We've lost the contract, Beth. He's signed with another vineyard.'

Beth stared at him, aghast.

'But, why? We have a quality product, our prices are competitive And he seemed so sure.'

'We're not competitive enough, apparently. He's signed with a rival of ours who has offered a lower price. Their vineyard isn't far from here. Juan knows the son quite well as it happens and, somehow, they seemed to know exactly what to offer to undercut us. That's quite some coincidence, isn't it?'

Beth felt suddenly cold.

'What are you implying?'

'Nothing. I'm asking you, Beth. Did you speak about this deal to Juan? Only, suddenly, one of his drinking pals knows enough about it to steal it from us. Were you responsible for that?'

Beth tried to keep her anger under control but it was difficult to stop resentment from welling up inside her at his accusatory tone.

'I have never said anything to Juan about confidential business matters,' she said icily. 'I wouldn't dream of such a thing.'

'Are you certain you let nothing slip inadvertently?' Vincente persisted. 'Only it's difficult to be on guard all the time, especially when you're involved with someone.'

'That might well be, but I have no conflict of interest in this case as I am not romantically linked to Juan,' Beth replied.

Vincente looked taken aback.

'That's not what you implied in Barcelona.'

Beth shook her head impatiently.

'There seems to have been some sort of misunderstanding but I fail to see what my private life has to do with our present discussion. The fact is, you have virtually accused me of passing on sensitive information. I have given you my word that I have always behaved with complete discretion. Is my word not good enough for you, Vincente?'

When he finally answered, every word was etched with scepticism.

'Only two people at Casa Perez knew the details of this transaction, Beth, you and I, and the leak certainly didn't come from me.'

'I see,' Beth said. 'In the circumstances, then, I believe I must resign.'

'There's no need to be hasty, Beth. We need to discuss this further.'

'No. You don't trust me. That makes working together impossible.'

She went to brush past him as one hand came grabbed her wrist.

'Wait! Don't go! I've been clumsy and boorish but if you'll give me a chance to explain.'

'It's too late for that.'

She pulled herself free with a downward thrust of her hand and then fled into the hallway with but one thought in her head, to leave Casa

Perez that instant. Without thinking through her resolution, she strode out of the front door, her vision blurred by the hot sting of tears. She was halfway down the driveway before it occurred to her that she had no money, no transport, and that all her belongings were still inside the house. She stopped abruptly, wondering if it would spoil her dramatic exit to go back and ask for a lift to the airport. The absurdity of her situation was not lost on her.

As she hesitated, a car drove in through the gates and came to a sudden halt beside her. The driver's door opened and a blonde head peered out.

'Beth! Darling!'

'Patrick! What on earth are you doing here?'

'Looking for you, of course. I've been searching for weeks.'

He climbed out of the car, and then stood looking down at her.

'I've come here to make it up to you for being such a brute and to take you back to England. Will you come back with me, darling?'

Beth looked up at him with widened blue eyes, knowing that now was not the time to question his motives, or his conduct.

'Oh, yes, please, take me home, Patrick,' she found herself saying.

When his arm went around her and she was pulled against him she didn't object and, when a familiar, imperious voice broke the silence, she remained within the circle of Patrick's arms.

'What is going on?' Vincente repeated.

He must have followed in the wake of her headlong flight from the house and was now standing before them, his expression stormy. Fortunately, Beth was saved from having to reply by Patrick.

'My name is Patrick Neal,' he said with his customary aplomb. 'I am Beth's fiancé and she has just agreed to return to England with me.'

8

Beth opened the door to her flat, deposited her bags of shopping and scooped up the postcard lying face upwards on the mat. The colourful Spanish setting proclaimed the sender even before Beth flipped it over to find Juanita's neat handwriting on the reverse. Deciding to read it over a coffee Beth went into her small kitchen to put on the kettle, and, as her eyes strayed to the window she couldn't help but contrast the postcard with the overcast sky which seemed to greet Londoners most days now that they had reached November.

After her departure from Casa Perez, Beth had found it difficult to settle back into normal routine and had thrown herself into the tasks of finding work and somewhere to live so that she would have less time to brood over the loss of her life in Spain. Patrick had tried to resolve her problems by offering her her old job back as his assistant and asking her to move into his apartment with him. She had turned down both offers in favour of doing temporary work and had been able to take over the lease of a flat from a girl who worked for the same agency as herself, who had gone aboard.

During their journey back from Spain, she and Patrick had managed a frank discussion on their situation. Her first task had been to explain why she had been so willing to return with him and then to make him understand that her co-operation did not mean she was willing to forgive his behaviour and accept him back into her life. On his part he had insisted that as soon as he had realised he had made a dreadful mistake, he had set out to rectify the situation, but Beth remained sceptical, pointing out that when he had broken their engagement he had left her stranded in Spain with little money and had only come in search of her when it suited him.

Finding that he was quite unable to breach the defences she was putting up against him, Patrick wondered silently what had happened in Spain to strengthen her resolve and make her so immune to his charm. Deciding to play a long-term game, he offered her friendship for the time being and she accepted, surprising herself with the ease with which she was able to handle the situation. Patrick had once seemed the centre of her universe, from prospective husband to friend, but things had changed for her at last.

As far as Beth was concerned, nothing of the old magic remained. Knowing he still had hopes of resurrecting a romance between them, she kept him at a friendly distance but rarely refused his invitations as he was lively company and evenings out with Patrick were often just what she needed to stop her brooding over what had happened in Spain.

The truth was that, not only did Beth miss her life at Casa Perez and the twins, but she found herself missing her infuriating boss as well! One consolation was that Juanita and Juan had kept in close contact and now, as Beth scanned her friend's postcard, she had a surprise in store. Juanita was coming to London! She would be in town the very next week and gave the telephone number of the hotel where she'd be staying. Delighted, Beth resolved to call her as soon as she arrived and arrange a meeting.

★　★　★

'Beth! How wonderful to see you.'

Juanita kissed her friend on both cheeks and then held her at arm's length, eyeing her critically.

'You look pale, my friend. You are missing the Spanish sun.'

'I always look pale,' Beth pointed out. 'But, you're right, I am missing the Spanish sun!'

They laughed and then Juanita caught the eye of a passing waiter and ordered tea for them both. They were in the comfortable lobby of Juanita's hotel and, as Beth settled back into the snug sofa, she assured her friend there was little to tell.

'Everything is much the same as when I last spoke to you on the phone. The agency is finding me plenty of well-paid work and that's wonderful as I need to find Grandmother's nursing home fees as well as support myself.'

'What about life outside work? Is Patrick still hoping to win you back?'

Beth had told her friend all about herself and Patrick during the many phone calls they had shared since her return home.

'I'm afraid so. I've been entirely honest with him but he still persists.'

'And is there no hope for you two? Are you quite unable to forgive him?'

'If I truly loved him I might be able to forgive his behaviour, but I doubt now that I ever was in love with him. I think I was just dazzled by his charm and good looks. That's no basis for a lasting relationship.'

'You sound sure of your feelings now, Beth, as though you really know yourself.'

'I know I don't want to marry Patrick, but that's all I am sure about. Anyway, how is Juan? Is there any news about his artistic ambitions?'

'There is the best news. Juan has been to see Senor Salzillo who has agreed to give him some private tuition. Then, if all goes well, Juan hopes to begin full-time study at the college where the senor teaches next year.'

She reached across to pat Beth on the hand.

'And it is thanks to you that this is happening. You could see that Juan was wasting his life and you did something about it. Our family owes you a debt, Beth, and I am just sorry that my obstinate cousin should repay you by throwing you out of our home.'

'It was I who decided to leave,' Beth

said, 'although I felt I had little choice once I had been accused of losing the company a lucrative deal.'

Juanita's shoulders rose.

'He is mad, my cousin. Juan knew nothing of that deal! I think Vincente knows now that he made a big mistake in blaming you. And if it helps, Beth, he is now paying the price for his foolishness.'

Beth felt a quickening of interest. She had heard little of Vincente since she had been in England and had to admit to herself that she was curious to know how he was faring. Badly, according to Juanita.

'He is like a bear with a sore head, as you English say. He has no assistant now and spends most of his time working. When we do see him at mealtimes he hardly speaks. Casa Perez has not been a happy place.'

'Doesn't Diane help to cheer him up? She always seemed happy to pander to his every whim.'

'Diane left the area shortly after you.

No-one seems to know where she went. She left a trail of unpaid bills behind her. It seems that the glamorous Diane was not as rich and successful as she liked to pretend.'

Diane's departure must be accounting for Vincente's low spirits, Beth surmised inwardly, and, unwilling to speculate further on the plight of her former boss, she made an effort to switch the conversation to something which had intrigued her since she had heard Juanita was coming to London.

'I've given you all my news,' she said, 'and we've discussed your relatives, so perhaps now we can talk about you. What exactly are you here for? It's lovely to see you, of course, but I have the distinct impression there's more to this then meets the eye.'

Smilingly Juanita brushed aside Beth's curiosity.

'It's just a shopping trip and to see you, that's all.'

Beth was unconvinced but the tea arrived just then and Juanita used the interruption to deflect her friend's curiosity with general chat. Afterwards, when she mulled over the encounter, Beth felt sure Juanita was holding something back but, as it happened, she had to wait several days before she was enlightened.

On Saturday mornings, Patrick had a habit of dropping by for coffee and when the doorbell caught Beth in the act of cleaning out the kitchen cupboards, she put the kettle on before hurrying to the door. To her surprise, Juanita was on the doorstep, looking jubilant.

'I can see you have some news for me. I was just making coffee so, come on, and tell me all about it,' Beth said.

When she returned to the living-room with the coffee tray, she found Juanita pacing about, obviously too keyed up even to sit down, and as Beth handed her a drink, she burst it out.

'I've got a job, Beth, here in London.'

'Oh, Juanita, that's wonderful. What will you be doing?'

'I'm to work for an old friend of my father's who works at the Spanish Embassy here and is a part-time historian. He wants me to do research for him which involves translating English documents into Spanish. I am sure I shall find it interesting, Beth.'

'And is this the secret you were hiding from me the other day?'

Juanita had the grace to blush.

'I didn't want to say anything until it was confirmed. Senor Peral asked me to work for him some time ago, when Father was alive, but Father refused to give me permission to come to London. Later on, when we had those conversations about what I should do with my life, I remembered the senor's job offer. I contacted him and he suggested I come here to talk things over. So that's what I did, and everything's worked out beautifully.'

'Will you be staying at the senor's house whilst you are in London?'

'No. I shall work from his house in Kensington but I shall have to find my own accommodation. Perhaps you can help me in that, Beth?'

Perhaps she could. A gem of an idea had been formulating whilst Juanita had been speaking and now she put it into words.

'I have a spare bedroom, you know, and this flat is quite large for one. What do you think about sharing with me? Oh, I know this place isn't anywhere near as grand as Casa Perez, but I'd make you very welcome.'

'Oh, Beth! What a wonderful idea! You really wouldn't mind sharing?'

At Beth's insistence that she would be delighted, Juanita's response was to give her friend a quick, fierce hug.

'Then I accept. We will have so much fun together.'

The doorbell rang once more and Beth rose to answer it.

'That'll be Patrick. He often joins me for coffee on a Saturday morning.'

After introducing him to her friend, Beth disappeared into the kitchen to brew more coffee and when she returned, it was to find Patrick speaking to Juanita in Spanish and exerting his usual charm as Juanita, dark eyes sparkling, fended off a compliment. She turned to Beth with a smile.

'Your friend has a wicked tongue, Beth. I shall have to be on my guard.'

'It's simply that I sound more impressive in Spanish,' Patrick claimed. 'I sound deadly dull in English and can't get any woman to take me seriously.'

This last comment was aimed at Beth but she did not rise to the bait and, as she listened to the lively banter developing between Juanita and Patrick, she found herself feeling a little surprised by her reaction. Her ex-fiancé was flirting with her friend in front of her and she felt nothing but indifference. Was this final proof that her romantic feelings for Patrick were truly over? Yes, answered her heart, without hesitation.

Juanita moved in a few days later. She had brought few possessions from

Spain with her and, in typical fashion, told Beth that she intended to treat herself to a new London wardrobe to mark the start of her new life. Beth's help was enlisted, but if she thought Juanita was going to build up a set of sober working clothes she was mistaken. Fearing that Senor Peral would react badly to Juanita turning up to work in some of the more outlandish garments she had chosen, Beth persuaded her to compromise by buying some conventional outfits as well.

'You will turn me into a proper working girl, yet,' Juanita announced as, later, she as unpacking her new clothes back at the flat. 'And I will listen to your advice, Beth, because I want to put the old Juanita behind me.'

'Well, don't change too much,' Beth said. 'I like you as you are.'

'But seriously,' Juanita said, sitting down on her bed, a frown creasing her brow, 'I do so much want to make a success of my new job. I'm a little afraid, Beth, afraid that I will fail.'

'Now look here,' Beth assured her as she sat beside her. 'Senor Peral has enough faith in you to offer you this job and he wouldn't have have such a successful career if he hadn't been a good judge of character. The least you can do is have the same sort of faith in yourself.'

'As usual you are right, my friend, and now I will stop feeling sorry for myself, put the rest of these clothes away, and then we will think about where we are going to dine this evening.'

Over the next few weeks, it became clear that Juanita's doubts about her ability to do her new job had been proved unfounded. She adored the translation work and developed an unexpected penchant for the research side of the job, confessing to Beth that she liked nothing better than to settle down with some dusty archive material in a library. Many of her working hours were spent in the senor's study in his house in Kensington and she quickly established a rapport with his family.

Senor Peral often hosted parties and receptions at his house for expatriate Spaniards living in London and Juanita was often invited to attend. At first, Beth accompanied her and then, increasingly, Patrick took on the rôle. Beth had watched with interest as the friendship between Patrick and Juanita blossomed, promising much more, and, keen to gauge her friend's feelings, Beth broached the subject one evening after dinner when they were relaxing with some coffee.

'You and Patrick seem to be getting along very well,' she observed.

Juanita's head lifted up from her glossy magazine.

'Oh, we're just friends. He has been very kind since I moved here. I think he wants me to feel at home.'

'I rather think it's more than kindness.'

Juanita snapped shut the magazine and sat upright on the sofa.

'Do you really think so? But how do

you feel about that, Beth? Not so long ago you were planning to marry him. I would never do anything to hurt our friendship, you know.'

'Well, growing closer to Patrick will not damage that,' Beth said firmly. 'I don't believe I was ever truly in love with Patrick, nor he with me, and can only be thankful that circumstances separated us.'

Juanita exhaled suddenly.

'It is such a relief to hear you say that! I have been so worried. You see, my feelings for Patrick seem to be growing stronger all the time. But am I wise to feel this way? After all, he did not behave well towards you.'

'No, he did not,' Beth replied. 'He proved himself to be very fickle. However, I've observed him since you two met and it's quite clear that he's been bowled over by you. I think you should follow your instincts, Juanita. There's no reason why you shouldn't be the woman to put Patrick's philandering ways behind him.'

Confirmation of Patrick's feelings towards Juanita came one evening when he came to take her out and found Beth alone as her friend had been delayed at work. Beth set about making him some coffee whilst he waited and he followed her into the kitchen, his manner noticeably distracted. She let him bide his time and, as she handed him his drink, he burst it out.

'I really need to get something off my chest, Beth.'

'Is this about you and Juanita?'

At his surprised look she continued.

'It's obvious by the way you look at her that you're crazy about her.'

'And I thought I was being cool about the whole thing! But, seriously,' he added, 'I value the friendship you and I have built up since we put our broken engagement behind us and I don't want anything to change that.'

'Neither do I,' she confirmed, 'and I don't believe your romance with Juanita will spoil anything, unless you treat her badly,' she added warningly.

'Ouch! I deserved that. I admit that my track record with women has not been good. I have every intention of changing that,' he stated solemnly.

'Well, just make sure you stick to that resolution.'

I sound just like some agony aunt, she thought suddenly. Perhaps my energies should be redirected towards resurrecting my own love life.

Ever since she had returned from Spain, Beth had been aware of an aching void in her life and, in a rare moment of self knowledge, she wondered if her unhappiness was less to do with the loss of a way of life than with the loss of one person — Vincente.

9

'Juan is to join us here for Christmas, Beth,' Juanita exclaimed one morning over breakfast.

Beth looked across the breakfast table at her friend.

'Isn't that good news? You sound rather doubtful about it.'

'I am. I fear he is coming to London to look into Vincente's background. You see, he's been more convinced lately by local gossip that Victoria, Vincente's mother, had a secret love affair before she returned to England and that Uncle Esteban was not the father of her child.'

'He suggested that to me once,' Beth confirmed. 'I told him that I didn't want to listen to tittle-tattle.'

'That's how I feel. Anyway, since I've been here doing research, Juan has asked me repeatedly to look up Vincente's birth certificate. He's sure it will not name Esteban as the father and thinks that, if he can prove that Vincente is not a blood relative, he will be in a better position to have our inheritance restored to us.'

'But do you want to go along with this?'

'No! I have refused to help him. I have a new life now, Beth, and my future lies here with Patrick. The last thing I want is to be dragged into the past, into useless, hurtful arguments about the Perez estate.'

Beth could see her point but felt she needed to be candid.

'You may be able to make a break with the past but, obviously, Juan feels differently. If he chooses to do some research there's little you can do about it. Surely you're not going to refuse to spend Christmas with him.'

'Of course not, we always spend Christmas together, but I'm not going to be drawn back into the family feud, Beth.'

'Well, make that quite clear to Juan

when he arrives,' Beth advised. 'And you never know, once Juan has done his research, and realised his theory is nonsense, it might encourage him to concentrate all his energies on his new life, as you are doing.'

'I can but live in hope, Beth, as you English say.'

When Juan did arrive, ten days before Christmas, there was little sign of disharmony between the twins. They hugged as though they had been apart for years. When it was Beth's turn to be greeted Juan held her at arm's length, appraising her critically.

'You are as beautiful as ever, Beth, but you are very pale and there is a sadness in your eyes. I think you have been missing me terribly.'

'I certainly haven't missed your modesty,' Beth exclaimed, laughing, but Juan took her teasing in good part, declaring that the glow would soon return to her cheeks now they were re-united.

It was pleasant to be back in his

company, Beth admitted to herself, and it was clear, from the enthusiastic way he described his studies with Senor Salzillo, that this new life was agreeing with him.

Over the next few days, Juan never mentioned Vincente once and seemed preoccupied with settling into his hotel and commandeering either Beth or Juanita to go sightseeing with him. Juanita was clearly pleased at this, but Beth experienced mixed feelings. She had had precious little news of Vincente since her stormy departure from his life and couldn't help feeling curious as to how he was faring.

'Senor Peral is holding one of his receptions tomorrow night, Beth,' Juan told her as they shared a late supper at the flat one evening. 'Juanita is going with Patrick so why don't you come with me? It should be fun.'

'Why not?' Beth replied, pleased at the prospect of a night out.

When the four of them assembled in the lobby of Senor Peral's large

Kensington house the following evening Beth was glad that she had taken pains with her appearance as they were surrounded by quite a crowd of elegantly-attired people. As they moved forward to hand in their invitations to the blue-liveried staff, Juan slipped her arm through his.

'I think I am going to enjoy tonight, Beth,' he whispered.

When Beth saw the appetising food, mostly Spanish delicacies, laid out she could only agree and as she drank the delicious Spanish wine brought to her by Juan and listened to the Spanish voices around her she could almost imagine herself back in the country which had come to mean so much to her. In time she and Juan drifted apart to circulate and Beth found herself talking, quite happily, to complete strangers who usually turned out to be colleagues of Senor Peral at the Spanish embassy. When an English voice spoke, her head shot round in surprise. It was Sheila Tennant.

'Why, Beth,' she repeated. 'How nice to meet up with you again.'

'And you,' Beth said, regaining her composure. 'Is your husband here?'

'Oh, he's about somewhere,' Mrs Tennant said vaguely, and there was an awkward pause before she went on to say, 'I know things didn't work out, business-wise, between your boss and my husband but you were very kind to me in Barcelona, and I'm grateful to you for that.'

'It was a pleasure,' Beth said, and meant it. 'Do you know Senor Peral well?' she asked, in an attempt at small talk.

'We don't know him at all,' Sheila confided. 'Diane Preston brought us tonight. We've become quite friendly since she's been advising us on business matters.'

'Diane Preston?' Beth repeated, a germ of a suspicion in her mind.

'Of course, you know her from Spain, don't you? Well, she's right over there if you want to say hello.'

Beth followed Sheila's gaze in time to see Diane turn and head for the door. After muttering her excuses, Beth followed in her wake, moving as quickly as possible through the crowd. Even so, as she left the reception, she was only just in time to see Diane sweep up to the double-fronted doors, leading to the street, which were about to be opened for her by a member of staff.

'Diane! Wait! We need to talk!'

She turned, her face breaking into a derisive smile at the sight of Beth.

'Why, if it isn't the little secretary. I have nothing to say to you.'

'If you don't speak to me now, in private, I'll make a scene right here.'

Diane looked from Beth to the curious eyes of the doorman, shrugged her shoulders and said, 'All right, what do you suggest?'

'In here.'

Beth jerked her head in the direction of a small cloak-room which she hoped was empty. She followed Diane in and slammed the door shut.

'I think you know what I want to ask you, Diane. Sheila Tennant has just alerted me to the business help you gave her husband. It was you who leaked details of Vincente's deal to his rivals, wasn't it?'

'Yes.'

As Beth stared at her, aghast at the arrogant admission, she elaborated further, seeming to take delight in her double-dealing.

'I was broke. None of my business ventures had taken off and I knew Vincente's competitors would pay well for information allowing them to gain an advantage. That office of yours was never locked so I went in and just took what I wanted. It was easy, honey, like taking candy from a baby.'

Beth could not rein in her indignation.

'But you were involved with Vincente. How could you betray him?'

To her surprise Diane threw her head back and laughed.

'I was never involved with Vincente!

Not from want of trying on my part, I can assure you, but I never could breach that man's defences! I was still hopeful, though, until you walked into his life.'

Diane moved closer, her eyes like cold steel as they cut into Beth.

'You were a nobody, yet he looked at you as he'd never looked at me. I won in the end, though. He blamed you for the leak and you left him high and dry! That was a bonus I hadn't bargained for! Now, if you'll step aside.'

Realising she had little choice but to comply, Beth moved away from the door, the contempt evident in her voice, though, when she said, 'I think you've told me everything I need to know, so I'll bid you goodbye with the fervent wish we never meet again.'

'I'll second that, honey.'

With these words she was gone, leaving Beth to mull over her extraordinary confession.

Later, back at the flat, she told the twins of Diane's treachery.

'And to think of all the hospitality we offered her at Casa Perez,' Juanita exclaimed in indignation. 'But why did she do such an awful thing, Beth?'

'For money,' Beth explained, unwilling to reveal the added motive of jealousy.

'And Vincente blamed you as well as me!' Juan put in. 'And then kicked you out of the house!'

'I left of my own accord,' Beth reminded him.

'Do not make excuses for him, Beth. It is time my cousin paid the price for his arrogant behaviour.' Turning to Juanita, he went on, 'I know you are not happy about this but I am determined to look into Vincente's background. I do not believe he is a Perez, and I intend to prove it!'

Juanita responded in Spanish and, as the conversation between them grew more heated, Beth crept away to bed, not wanting to intrude on private family matters.

She had to work late the following

day and when she arrived home she found Juanita sitting alone. As soon as she caught sight of her face she knew something was wrong.

'In spite of my pleas Juan went out this morning determined to obtain a copy of Vincente's birth certificate,' Juanita explained. 'But that was hours ago, Beth. Where is he and what has he found out?'

Beth could offer little in the way of comfort but, in order to keep her friend occupied, suggested she help her prepare supper. They had just finished eating when the sound of the outer door opening and closing sent both of them hurrying into the living-room. Juan was standing there.

'I think you two had better sit down,' he said at the sight of them.

They did as he requested and, in spite of the many questions bubbling to her lips, Beth remained silent as Juan took his wallet out of his jacket pocket and removed a slip of paper.

'This is a copy of Vincente's birth

certificate. It names the father and I was right when I said it would not be Uncle Esteban, but wrong when I said Vincente was not a Perez.'

He handed the paper to Juanita and, eyes wide, she read it.

'But it names Felipe Perez as the father. What does this mean?' she gasped.

'It means that Vincente is, in fact, our elder brother. Father must have known that, Juanita, and that's why he made him his heir.'

Beth sensed the shock felt by Juanita and shared it. She had never felt comfortable with the idea of delving into such personal family matters but perhaps it was fitting that the twins should know the truth at last.

'I've been walking the streets for hours trying to sort out my feelings,' Juan went on, 'and I think the best thing for us both, Juanita, is to go back to Casa Perez and talk things through with Vincente. What do you think?'

'I agree,' Juanita replied, then she

turned anxiously to Beth. 'But what about you, Beth? It's not long to Christmas. Would you mind if we deserted you?'

Beth brushed aside her concerns.

'Certainly not. I think Juan is right. The sooner you two start talking to Vincente the better. Don't worry about me. I'll be fine.'

The twins left the next day. Immediately, Beth began to miss their lively company but consoled herself with the thought that their trip home might mark the final end of a bitter family feud.

Juanita phoned a few days later.

'I'll save explanations until we can tell you in person but everything is going well. In fact, we've decided to stay for Christmas. Patrick is flying over to join us so why don't you come, too? We'd love to have you here, Beth.'

And I'd love to come, Beth thought, a sudden image of Vincente filling her mind's eye, but she knew what her answer had to be.

'I'm really sorry, but I'll have to refuse,' she went on. 'You see, I always spend Christmas morning with Gran. I should feel terrible if I weren't there for her at Christmas.'

'I understand,' Juanita replied. 'Take care of yourself, Beth, and we'll speak soon.'

The line went dead and Beth replaced the receiver with a heavy heart. The thought of Christmas lunch, alone here at the flat, did not appeal, but Beth knew she had done the right thing in refusing the invitation. After all the love and care Gran had lavished on her throughout her life it was a small sacrifice to make.

On the afternoon of Christmas Day, having visited her gran, the taxi deposited Beth on the pavement in front of her flat and, as she searched in her purse for her key, she gave her first thoughts to what she would eat for lunch. Not being in a festive mood she had not bought in anything special and was just wondering what was in the freezer when she stepped into the hall and was met by the strains of music coming from the living-room.

The twins must have come back after all! She hurried through and, at the sight of the dining table, came to a sudden halt. Set for two, it was clothed in a crimson table cloth with festive green trimmings and an ice bucket, containing what looked like a bottle of champagne, taking pride of place in the centre.

'We decided that, as you wouldn't come to us for Christmas, Beth, we should bring Christmas to you.'

She whirled round to find Vincente framed in the doorway leading to the kitchen. Her heart somersaulted and, in that instant, she knew why his face had haunted her dreams for so long. She had a crazy desire to run to him but instead spoke shakily.

'Is this part of some conspiracy?'

'Certainly,' he said with a dangerous edge to his voice.

Deftly he opened the champagne,

poured some into a tall, stemmed glass and then held it out to her.

'A peace offering, Beth. I should never have doubted you for one moment and I apologise from the bottom of my heart,' then, as she took the glass, he added, 'If it's any consolation, I realised quite soon after you had left that it was Diane who must have betrayed me. I was left to face the unpalatable truth that, through my own foolish actions, I had allowed her to win by driving from me the one woman I cared about.'

'But you could have contacted me, Vincente.'

He brushed one impatient hand through his dark hair.

'Beth, during these last, lonely weeks, I've thought of nothing but you. I've longed to see you, but I thought you and Patrick had got back together. When you left Casa Perez he declared himself to be your fiancé and I had no reason to believe otherwise until Juanita told me the true situation. Until then I thought I'd lost you for ever. But tell me, after all the crazy mistakes I've made, is there any hope that you can ever care for me?'

Her upturned face gave him the answer he craved and, as his lips met hers, they were lost for the moment in the magic of their reconciliation.

As his lips left hers he said shakily, 'I was drawn to you right from the start, you know, but I decided to tread warily as I knew you had just suffered a broken engagement. Then Juan seemed to be snatching you from me and, just as I was finally realising there was nothing between you, we have a terrible row and the next moment you are walking off with Patrick Neal!'

'We haven't made it easy for ourselves,' Beth admitted. 'I was convinced you were involved with Diane.'

'Love has a way of making us crazy, darling, but there's no need to hold back now.'

Just as his lips were reaching for hers again the doorbell rang. He drew back with a rueful comment.

'Bad timing! That will be the caterers. I'm afraid my culinary skills don't stretch to Christmas lunch!'

'It's not bad timing.' Beth smiled. 'I'm starving!'

Over a delicious meal Vincente spoke of the complex family matters uncovered recently by Juan.

'I only learned who my true parents were when some old family letters I came across alerted me, and my mother finally told me the truth. She and Felipe had fallen in love when she was an au pair and had planned to marry but his parents threatened him with disinheritance if he married someone they considered beneath him. Heartbroken, my mother returned home to England without telling Felipe that she was carrying his child. In due course I was born and my mother was joined in England by Esteban. He had loved her, too, and finally persuaded her to marry him. Not wanting the truth to come out, they distanced themselves from the family in Spain and I was brought up to believe that Esteban was in fact my father. I couldn't have wished for a better upbringing, Beth, but once I'd discovered everything I felt an overwhelming need to meet my natural father and siblings.

'Anyway, I decided to visit Casa Perez, without revealing the truth about myself, of course, but it wasn't long before Felipe guessed the truth. Even so, I was as surprised as everyone else when I found out he'd made me his heir. It was a difficult decision, Beth, but I decided in the end to accept my natural father's wishes and take over Perez Vineyards. I knew I could make a success of it and, as the twins had no real interest in winemaking, I hoped that a generous settlement would ease their sense of grievance.'

'But why didn't you tell them the truth?' Beth asked. 'They just thought their father had rejected them.'

'I longed to tell them the truth but it wasn't my decision. My mother and

Esteban, the man who had brought me up as a loving father, did not want anyone else to know what had happened. I had to respect their wishes.'

Of course he'd had to remain silent and Beth's heart swelled with sympathy at the difficult choices he'd faced.

'The changed will certainly soured relations between you and the twins, but what about now?' she asked. 'Now that they know you are their half-brother, do you think you will be able to be reconciled with them?'

'I believe so. We have had long discussions since they returned to Spain with their new-found knowledge. We are on the way to a new understanding. Of course,' he added, mischievously, 'our reconciliation would be greatly helped if I were to marry one of their best friends.'

Beth's heart seemed to stop and she found herself saying, shakily, 'I'm always willing to help out my friends.'

'Good, because you already have my heart, Beth, and now I hope you will take my hand as well. Will you marry me and help to bring the same harmony to my life that you have already brought to my family?'

'Gladly,' Beth said, as she reached out to him.

THE END

We do hope that you have enjoyed reading this large print book.

Did you know that all of our titles are available for purchase?

We publish a wide range of high quality large print books including:
Romances, Mysteries, Classics
General Fiction
Non Fiction and Westerns

Special interest titles available in large print are:
The Little Oxford Dictionary
Music Book, Song Book
Hymn Book, Service Book

Also available from us courtesy of Oxford University Press:
Young Readers' Dictionary
(large print edition)
Young Readers' Thesaurus
(large print edition)

For further information or a free brochure, please contact us at:
Ulverscroft Large Print Books Ltd.,
The Green, Bradgate Road, Anstey,
Leicester, LE7 7FU, England.
Tel: (00 44) **0116 236 4325**
Fax: (00 44) **0116 234 0205**

SUMMER IN HANOVER SQUARE

Charlotte Grey

The impoverished Margaret Lambart is suddenly flung into all the glitter of the Season in Regency London. Suspected by her godmother's nephew, the influential Marquis St. George, of being merely a common adventuress, she has, nevertheless, a brilliant success, and attracts the attentions of the young Duke of Oxford. However, when the Marquis discovers that Margaret is far from wanting a husband he finds he has to revise his estimate of her true worth.

CONFLICT OF HEARTS

Gillian Kaye

Somerset, at the end of World War I: Daniel Holley, unhappily married to an ailing wife and father of four grown-up children, is attracted to beautiful schoolteacher Harriet Bray, but he knows his love is hopeless. Daniel's only daughter, Amy, who dreams of becoming a milliner and is caught up in her love for young bank clerk John Tottle, looks on as the drama of Daniel and Harriet's fate and happiness gradually unfolds.

THE SOLDIER'S WOMAN

Freda M. Long

When Lieutenant Alain d'Albert was deserted by his girlfriend, a replacement was at hand in the shape of Christina Calvi, whose yearning for respectability through marriage did not quite coincide with her profession as a soldier's woman. Christina's obsessive love for Alain was not returned. The handsome hussar married an heiress and banished the soldier's woman from his life. But Christina was unswerving in the pursuit of her dream and Alain found his resistance weakening . . .

THE TENDER DECEPTION

Laura Rose

When Sophia Barton was taken from Curton Workhouse to be a scullery-maid at Perriman Court, her future looked bleak. Was it really an act of Providence that persuaded Lady Perriman to adopt her as her ward? Sophia was brought up together with the Perriman children, and before sailing with his regiment for India, George, the heir to the title, declared his love. But tragedy hit the family and Sophia found herself caught up in a web of mystery and intrigue.

CONVALESCENT HEART

Lynne Collins

They called Romily the Snow Queen, but once she had been all fire and passion, kindled into loving by a man's kiss and sure it would last a lifetime. She still believed it would, for her. It had lasted only a few months for the man who had stormed into her heart. After Greg, how could she trust any man again? So was it likely that surgeon Jake Conway could pierce the icy armour that the lovely ward sister had wrapped about her emotions?